LADY ANNE'S DECEPTION

LADY ANNE'S DECEPTION

'Somehow I will marry before Marigold – anyone who will have me'.

When Lady Anne Sinclair vowed to marry before her sister, she had no idea the 'anyone' would be the Marquess of Torrance. The darling of the town – and considered the most confirmed bachelor until he succumbed to Annie's charms.

But Annie's battle for attention had ill-prepared her for married life. In a tipsy revery on her wedding night, she blurted out her real reason for marrying the Marquess – and her husband's pride shut the door on any further communication.

OTHER MARION CHESNEY TITLES IN LARGE PRINT

Lady Anne's Deception

by
Marion Chesney

MAGNA PRINT BOOKS
Long Preston, North Yorkshire,
England.

OCT 2 7 1994

4

British Library Cataloguing in Publication Data

Chesney, Marion
   Lady Anne's deception.

A CIP catalogue record for this book is available from the British Library.

ISBN 07505 0153 7

First Published in Great Britain 1991 by Severn House Publishers Ltd.

Copyright © 1985 by Marion Chesney.

Published in Large Print 1992 by arrangement with Severn House Publishers Ltd.

Printed and bound in Great Britain by T.J. Press (Padstow) Ltd.

For
Marion and John Leslie
With Love

Chapter One

SOMETIMES circumstances, our peers, and our betters force us into a role that at first we don't want to play. But after a time it becomes a habit.

Take the plight of Lady Annie Sinclair, youngest daughter of the Earl of Crammarth. All she seemed to hear was "Annie is such a *sensible* little thing. Not a beauty like Marigold. But then she has *brains*."

This view was held by her mother, the countess, the servants, her grim old nanny, and her vague governess. What her father, the earl, though of her was a mystery. Annie sometimes wondered if he knew she existed.

Inside, she knew herself to be dreamy and romantic. But gradually, on the outside, she came to behave the way that was expected of her. She was never Anne, always Annie – practical, level-headed little Annie. Lady Marigold, her sister, was a beauty to break hearts. Everyone assumed that Marigold, therefore, had a beautiful soul, and did not seem to notice that she was spoiled almost past reclaim.

Annie had been born in the castle of Crammarth, a romantic, chilly barn of a place, but, for all that, it was a place to dream in. Three years ago the earl had taken his family to their town house in Edinburgh while the castle was razed to the ground and replaced by a modern, neo-Georgian structure that was warm, luxurious, and ugly.

He had just moved them all back again into the new house, and life was an endless succession of house parties where guests exclaimed over "how up-to-date" everything was.

Annie was eighteen years of age and her sister, Marigold, nineteen. Marigold had masses of that nut-brown color of hair that was so fashionable and wide blue eyes set in a heart-shaped face. Her skin was perfect, and her hourglass figure owed nothing to art or padding. She was slightly above average height and moved with willowy grace.

Annie was small and wiry. She, too, had large eyes, but they were gray and made her small face seem thinner than it was. She was neat and brisk in her movements.

Her hair was red. It was not copper or Titian or auburn. It was plain red, without the usual coarse quality that goes with that color.

Fine and silky, it kept falling loose from its pins when she experimented putting her hair up. Nanny Simpkins said crossly that it was just as well that Annie had not made her coming-out and therefore could not wear her hair up.

Nanny Simpkins was full of remarks like that. She was one of those irritating old family retainers who hide behind the role of "character" so that no one quite noticed that she was just plain rude. "Our dear Simpers," the countess called her. "So wise."

The Earl and Countess of Crammarth had married when the earl was forty-five and his bride, thirty. The earl's friends were mostly middle-aged or elderly, and so there were very few young men at the endless house parties. Those that did come were too interested in the earl's excellent shooting, hunting, and fishing to pay much attention to the females of the house.

At last the house parties stopped. It was the middle of winter and a great silence lay over the frozen countryside. Frost rimmed the leaves of the evergreens in the drive, furred the shaggy grass of the lawn, and glittered on the long, brown snakes of the plowed fields. The sky was leaden and the ornamental lake like polished steel.

Wrapped in a long tweed coat, with her head covered by a repellent black felt hat, Annie was skirting the edge of the home wood, luxuriating in the peace and quiet. When she returned home, there would be no hearty guests to entertain. Mama had even said that, just for this one evening, they would not bother dressing for dinner.

Annie liked being alone. She felt that she could drop the character that had been manufactured for her and dream in peace. Dream all those lovely romantic dreams of love and marriage.

The house shone with a horrible newness against the soft folds of the Perthshire countryside. No Georgian would have recognised it, neo or not. It was a huge, sprawling edifice with steep, tiled roofs and huge bay windows, rather like shop windows, on the ground floor. Little circular windows had been cut into the stone at random on the upper floors, no doubt to give the supposed Georgian effect.

It was very cold. The deer nuzzled at bundles of hay on the grass. The sky was a uniform gray. The birds were silent. Thin columns of smoke rose from the chimneys, straight up into the frosty air. Her boots left neat, little, pointed footprints on the whitened grass.

Suddenly a great wind seemed to spring out of nowhere and set the landscape to dancing. Little frozen waves with miniature whitecaps raced across the surface of the lake. The deer tossed their heads and scampered for safety. A cloud of rooks rose from the trees and wheeled against the darkening sky. The branches of the trees above her head moaned and rattled in the wind. And then snow began to fall, hissing down on the hard ground, falling in tiny frozen pellets, whipping through the bushes and across the lawns, falling faster until the house was almost lost to her view.

Annie huddled into her coat and began to hurry home.

She could never enter the new house without a small feeling of shock. In the old castle, a huge open fire would have been blazing in the hall. But this new hall only had a small fire burning in a tiny grate under an enormous pilastered mantelpiece that looked like a piece of a church, soaring in all its chilly mahogany glory to the ceiling as if it had nothing to do with the little blaze at its feet.

She gave her hat and coat to the butler and went into the drawing room where the family gathered for their predinner sherry. Marigold was pouting in a corner; her mother and father were arranged in front of the fireplace —

pseudo-Adam – as if posing for their portrait; Nanny Simpkins was snoring over her knitting in an easy chair by the window; and Miss Higgins, the governess, with her habitual look of an anxious rabbit, eyes and teeth protruding, was standing in the coldest corner of the cold room.

And the drawing room *was* cold. The lower part of the walls were of deep blue, glazed tiles, and the floor was of green and white marble.

The architect had flattered the earl by suggesting that his lordship's collection of souvenirs from his travels in the South Seas be displayed in glass cases in the drawing room. And so it was rather like sipping sherry in a museum. Sinister little carved gods with quite enormous phalluses stared out through the glass at the family. Marigold and Annie did not find these carvings in the least embarrassing, merely thinking that the gods of the South Seas were mysteriously endowed with an extra leg.

The absence of guests made Annie realize anew how very silent her parents were. The earl was a small, stout man with an enormous waxed moustache and a monocle in one eye. His sparse gray hair was carefully greased and combed over his bald spot. The countess was a stately woman with a sculptured figure. Her face bore the lines of years of discontent. At one time she had been a great beauty, like her daughter Marigold.

It was only during the past year that the girls had been allowed to join their parents for dinner. Before that they had had nursery tea with Nanny and the governess in the school-room. When they were considered old enough for dinner, somehow Nanny and the governess came, too, provided there were no guests.

The earl and the countess prided themselves on never retiring a servant, and quite a number of the staff were old and creaky. Annie felt privately that it would have been more humane to have pensioned some of them off.

"I've been thinkin', " began the earl. Annie looked up in surprise. His voice sounded very loud in the silent, chilly room. "Marigold here should be thinkin' of gettin' married."

Marigold's pout became more pronounced. "Who to, Papa?" she drawled. "Everyone who comes here's in his dotage."

Coming from Annie, a remark like that would have been treated as the height of impertinence. But no one ever listened to Marigold. They only looked.

"So Lady Crammarth and I have decided to send Marigold to London for a season. That's

15

where the money is." The earl always gave his wife her title, even when talking to his daughters.

"London," breathed Marigold, her pout disappearing among the dimples.

"Of course, Annie will go with you. Not much hope of her makin' a good marriage, but she's got her head screwed on the right way and she'll see you don't run off with anyone unsuitable, Marigold."

"But I'm older than she is and I'm quite able to take care of myself," protested Marigold.

"You can't have everything," her father said reasonably. "You've got the looks and Annie's got the brains. The fact is, a good marriage would be just the thing. All this entertaining's cost more than I ever imagined it would. Lady Crammarth won't be bringin' you out. Your Aunt Agatha will be doin' the honors."

"Oh, goodie!" cried Marigold, clapping her hands while Annie's heart plummeted down to her button boots.

Aunt Agatha, Miss Agatha Winter, was a lacquered fashion plate of a woman who patronized Annie quite dreadfully on her mercifully infrequent visits north.

Dinner was an animated affair that evening for all but Annie.

16

Marigold basked in the admiration of her small court. Nanny Simpkins swore that she would be engaged to a duke before the first month of the Season was over; Miss Higgins, the governess, smiled mistily and prophesied that Marigold would be the reigning belle and men would stand up in their carriages in the park to see her going past as they had done for Lilly Langtry, the Jersey Lily. The earl leaned forward to pat Marigold's curls. Only the countess seemed to feel that Annie was being left out of things and comforted her daughter with the remark, "Of course, when all this fuss is over, I'll be delighted to have you back with me again, Annie. You are *such* a help in running the house!"

The dining room was as cold as the drawing room had been, and Annie felt her future was as bleak as the weather had been that day. Until this moment, she had not realized how very bored she was with the dull routine of her days.

By the time Annie and her sister retired to the school-room, as was their custom after dinner, Annie's head was aching and she longed to run away to her bedroom and escape between the covers of the bed and the cover of one of the latest romances.

But Marigold wanted an audience. She

17

flopped down in a chintz-covered armchair and thrust her legs out in front of her and stared at the pointed toes of her openwork shoes. "At last!" she exclaimed. "I thought I would end up married to some creaking septuagenarian. To think of all my beauty being wasted on this desert air." She raised her eyes to Annie, who was standing by the fireplace, poised for flight. "Oh, sit down, *do*! You're always scampering about, Annie. Do you know why Papa has decided on this move?"

"Well, I suppose he thinks you're of an age to get married," she Annie.

"No. He wants me to marry a rich man because he's spent so much money on this dump and on entertaining all his senile friends, that he's run into debt."

"Oh, come, Marigold, some of his friends are very nice and not all that old. Anyway, what makes you think he's in debt? Papa never discusses money."

"I listened at their bedroom door last night and I heard Papa telling Mama." Marigold giggled. "You'd never guess what the old dears get up to in there. Quite sweet, really. Why, only the other night . . ."

"Marigold!" Annie's eyes were wide with shock. "You shouldn't listen at doors."

"Who are you to tell me what not to do,

Miss Prunes and Prisms? I shall pinch you for that."

Annie tried to escape, but her stronger sister had hurtled out of the armchair and seized her by the arm.

"Let me go!" Annie twisted in Marigold's grasp.

"I'll pinch you, and pinch you, and pinch you," said Marigold, suiting the action to the words.

Annie seized her sister's golden hair and gave it a hard tug. To her relief, Marigold immediately let go and started to sob.

"How dare you, Lady Annie!" cried Miss Higgins from the doorway. Annie sighed. She should have known that Marigold's about-face was because she had seen the governess.

"I don't know why you can't be more like your sister," Miss Higgins went on. "Of course, it must be upsetting to know that the family's hopes are pinned on Lady Marigold making a successful marriage. But you must count your blessings, Lady Annie, and thank God for what he has seen fit to give you. Your turn will come, I am sure."

"Oh, don't prose on so, Higgins," said Marigold, with sudden spite. "Can't I talk to my sister without having to listen to your moralizing? *You* won't be coming with us,

19

anyway. I'll make sure of that."

The end of Miss Higgins's long nose twitched with embarrassment.

"Don't be nasty, Marigold," said Annie.

"Lady Marigold was not being nasty," said Miss Higgins. "Lady Marigold was merely expressing her views."

"Good-bye," murmured Marigold, with a lazy smile.

Miss Higgins fled.

With one of her mercurial changes of mood, Marigold turned a winning smile on her sister. "Don't let's quarrel, Annie. Let's talk about *men*." She seized a copy of a glossy magazine and opened it to a well-thumbed page. "Now there's a man I would like to meet. The Marquess of Torrance."

Annie looked at the black-and-white photographs. Blank or startled well-bred faces stared at the camera. In one photograph was the Marquess of Torrance. He was talking to a willowy young lady whose face was almost concealed by the shadow thrown by her enormous cartwheel hat. He was laughing. His face seemed alive with mischief. He had very thick dark hair and a strong, handsome face.

"He might be married," ventured Annie.

"He's not. He's a terrible ladies' man, very wild, and quite the catch of the Season."

20

Annie studied the photograph again, her fine red hair falling in a curtain about her face. "He doesn't look all that young."

"I looked him up in the Peerage. He's thirty."

"There must be something up with him if he's not married," Annie said with a frown.

"He hasn't *had* to get married. He's had lots and lots of lady-loves. The actress, Viola Delaney, is said to have tried to kill herself when he left her. Don't you ever read the gossip columns? No, of course you don't. You're such a prude, Annie. It's not that you're precisely plain. It's just that you've always got a disapproving look – like a school-teacher. You would have made a better Higgins than Higgins."

"You're very cruel to Miss Higgins – and to Nanny, considering they dote on you."

"Oh, that's because I'm beautiful," said Marigold smugly. "You don't need to bother being nice when you're beautiful."

"But what about getting old?" asked Annie. "Have you thought of that? Have you thought of a husband who's become all too accustomed to your beauty? Think about it! I can see you now, lying on the chaise longue with your face in a chin-bracer, studying your wrinkles in the glass while your husband pays court to the latest beauty."

"Cat," said Marigold. "You're jealous. There's time enough to think about being charming and all that when I get a husband."

Marigold's beautiful eyes were suddenly bright with malice. "What's going on inside that carrot top? I know. You've been reading romances again, where the plain, little, bluestocking Cinderella attracts the dashing hero with her common sense. Rubbish! If there's one thing a man can't stand, it's an intelligent woman."

"Then you should have plenty of suitors," Annie flashed back, humiliated by the ease with which her sister had outlined one of her favorite fantasies.

Marigold stretched lazily. "I shall. Oh, indeed I shall. Now, why don't you run along to bed as you've been dying to do? The only romance you're going to find, precious little Annie, is between the cover of that book you've got hidden under your pillow."

Annie stood over her sister, her hands clenched. "You've been rummaging among my things. You have no . . ."

"But it's such fun." Marigold giggled. " 'Dear Diary, Nothing has happened today. Nothing ever happens. But one day *he* will come and I will recognize . . .' *Ow!*"

Outraged, Annie was shaking her as hard as she could. Marigold rolled out of the armchair and pulled Annie down to the floor by grabbing her ankles. Both rolled, bit, and scratched until at last Annie, for once, managed to get the upper hand by taking handfuls of her sister's hair and banging her head against the floor.

Abruptly, she released her and sat back on her heels, laughing. "What would the Marquess of Torrance say if he could see us now?" she gasped. Seeing Marigold was ready to continue the fight, she escaped along the corridor to her own room and locked the door.

Predictably, wild and noisy sobbing started to emanate from the schoolroom, then there was a loud banging on Annie's door and Nanny Simpkins shouted, "You open the door this minute, my lady. Your jealousy has gone too far. Poor Lady Marigold is quite distraught. Open the door, I say."

"Shan't," said Annie, sitting on her bed and clenching her fists. It was the first time she had ever got the better of Marigold in a fight and she was sure it would be the last.

There was a long silence. Then came Nanny's grim voice. "I have no other alternative but to tell your mother."

Annie shuddered. Her mother rarely interfered in the schooling of her daughters, but when she did the punishment was long and severe.

As Nanny's footsteps retreated, Annie grimly remembered all the humiliations she had suffered at Marigold's hands.

A sudden, terrible ambition was born in her breast. "Somehow," Lady Annie said aloud to herself, "I will marry before Marigold – to anyone who'll have me. Just so long as I get to the altar before her."

Chapter Two

MISS AGATHA WINTER was the Countess of Crammarth's sister, the countess having been a plain Miss Winter of the untitled aristocracy before she married the earl.

Aunt Agatha had never married. She had told so many people that she, Agatha, had been a great beauty in her youth that she had almost begun to believe it herself. She liked to hint at a great romance and a subsequent broken heart. She enameled her face white and painted red circles on her cheeks. Her fair hair was on the brassy side. Her dresses were always of clinging materials, and, given the slightest chance, she would wear the lowest-cut gowns possible, exposing an acreage of painted neck and bosom. Most of the time she looked like a badly stretched canvas.

In a lower circle of society, she would be condemned for dressing and making-up like a tart, but in the rarified heights of the London Season, she merely became one with the other raddled chaperones who lined the walls.

Her instructions from her sister were perfectly clear. Marigold must marry money. She was to be encouraged to smile on any suitor with a large bank balance and a desire to have a titled wife. If worst came to worst, an American would do, although young American males seemed to enjoy the spectacle of the London Season and then promptly went home to marry American girls. But then foreigners are so unaccountable. As Miss Winter's friend, Miss Shuttleworth-Snyde-Crimp, had said only the other day, "Perhaps *not* an American. The English names have gone from that country, and they now have such peculiar surnames as Bloomberger or something."

Miss Winter's home was as enameled as its owner. She had followed the vogue for painting furniture, and most of it was enameled a glaring white. Annie reflected that it was rather like making one's debut from a hospital ward.

The start of the Season was now barely a week away. According to the calendar, it was late spring. According to the fickle English weather, it was still winter.

Rain beat down on the muddy streets, and a great wind sent the cowls on the chimney stacks spinning. Cab horses shivered under sodden blankets as they waited at the ranks. You awoke to darkness, and by three in the afternoon the gas was already being lit. London seemed doomed to lie forever under a great flying bank of low, black clouds.

Miss Winter lived in a thin-walled house in Manchester Square. Damp permeated every room, and little beads of condensation slid down the chilly white of the furniture. She did not believe in lighting fires after the first of March, and so all of the fireplaces had on their summer dress of crêpe paper and pine cones under mantels draped in white lace.

One evening the enterprising Marigold had taken an axe to a chair in her bedroom and had invited Annie along to enjoy the blaze in the fireplace.

Miss Winter had promptly deducted the cost of the chair from Marigold's pin money and this punishment had drawn the sisters into a temporary friendship, like two warriors resting on their lances before the next battle.

Annie had been furious with Marigold all the way to London. Her punishment, meted out by the countess, had been a week on bread and water. But now she and Marigold were drawn together against the uncomfortable parsimony of their aunt and their mutual disappointment with London.

Annie did not know what Marigold had expected, but she had painted a picture of light, airy streets where ladies in beautiful, colored dresses moved gracefully like swans.

The reality was of scuttling figures dressed in gray and black and brown; damp clothes, damp smells, overflowing drains, and mud, mud, mud.

Annie had even accepted with equanimity that Marigold was to have the finer gown for the opening ball at Lady Trevelyn's mansion, Lady Trevelyn being one of the social leaders. Miss Winter had chosen Marigold's ball gown herself, and then she had turned Annie over to the care of the dressmaker, telling her that she could have whatever she wanted as long as she kept it within the stipulated price.

The meals, *chez* Winter, were abominable: cheap cuts of meat, soggy vegetables, stodgy puddings. Miss Winter instructed both girls to eat as much as possible during the Season – at other people's houses, of course.

On the day of the ball, Annie turned over in bed and buried her head under the bedclothes. She was tired of sitting up and looking out of the oblong window at that weeping gray sky every morning when the maid entered to draw the curtains.

She heard the maid's soft step and then the clink of china as her morning cup of tea and a plate with two Osborne biscuits were placed on the table beside her bed. Then the curtains were drawn.

And Annie became aware of a new sound. Birds were squabbling and chattering outside the window. Somewhere down in the square a barrel organ was grinding out a wheezy waltz.

She poked her head above the bedclothes and stared disbelievingly at the shaft of sunlight cutting an oblong across the polished boards.

And then her stomach began to churn with anticipation at the thought of the ball. But she no longer thought of finding a husband just to spite her sister. She had enjoyed their new closeness. It had made the discomforts of the Winter household seem almost worth bearing.

It was a kaleidoscope of a day. One moment it seemed as if the evening would never come, and then all at once it was rushing in upon her.

A lady's maid, Barton, had been hired to take care of Marigold and Annie, Miss Winter not wishing to pay for her services a day earlier than was necessary.

Both girls were to wear their hair up for the first time. The hairdresser arrived, tut-tutted over Annie's straight, fine, red hair, and then went to work, heating curling tongs over a spirit stove and filling the house with the scent of hot air.

The dress, which Annie had chosen at the dressmaker's urging, was in the new, sweet-pea color. It was made of clinging chiffon and seemed to float about her slim body. The neckline was deep, and the gown was secured at each shoulder by two frivolous bows that looked like wings. The skirt fell in beautifully scalloped layers of delicate chiffon, ending in a short spoon train at the back.

Her only ornament was a gold locket suspended on a thin chain, containing two pictures of her pony, Arnold. Young girls were not supposed to wear much jewelry, anyway. Married ones, however, were allowed to deck themselves out like jewelers' display trays.

After the hairdresser had finished, Barton appeared to help Annie with her corsets and gown.

At last it was time to look in the looking glass, time to see if she had turned into a woman. Annie had hoped that the lady's maid would make some comment, but Barton was quick, efficient, and silent.

She cautiously approached the long pier glass and found a stranger looking back at her. Her red hair was set high on her head in intricate swirls and loops and curls, and threaded with pearls. It was burnished like a flame. Her eyes looked enormous in her face, which had been delicately colored with rouge. The gown, padded at the bust and hips, made her tiny waist seem smaller than ever. The gown itself was like a spring symphony with the delicate pastel colors glowing in the light of the oil lamp.

The door opened and Marigold walked in. She was attired in a fussy debutante gown of white lace. Her beautiful golden hair had been fashionably frizzed at the front, rather giving her the look of a French poodle.

"Well, you *do* look a mess," she said slowly, surveying Annie with hard, bright eyes.

"Lady Marigold!" exclaimed Barton, startled into speech.

"Every young lady is going to be wearing white," Marigold went on, undeterred. "And you'll look like a freak. Whoever heard of a girl going to her first ball in *colors*?"

Annie studied her reflection in the glass. "No, Marigold," she said. "I'm not going to listen to you. I've never looked better in my life."

"That's not saying much," sneered Marigold. Then she turned on a charming smile. "Look, I really don't want you to make a fool of yourself. I've got another white ball gown I can let you have."

"No," said Annie, mutinously. "This is the first time I've looked attractive and I'm going to enjoy it."

Marigold gave a shrill laugh. "*You!* Look attractive! Take another look in the mirror. Oh, you've changed a little for the better, I'll admit. But you're still the insignificant little thing you always were!" She flounced out of the room.

Annie looked miserably at the glass, waiting for Barton to reassure her. But Barton had already grasped the fact that Marigold was the favored one and she did not want to lose her position. She mutely held out Annie's cloak and helped her into it.

Aunt Agatha was waiting with Marigold in the drawing room. She made no comment about Annie's appearance but praised Marigold so fulsomely that she quite restored that young lady to good humor.

As the open landau carried them through the streets during the early evening, Annie began to feel a recurring surge of anticipation and excitement. This was the London she had expected! The air was warm and sweet with a gray-and-rose twilight glowing behind the sooty houses. People strolled by, enjoying the soft evening air, and the ladies seemed to have blossomed into all the colors of the rainbow.

As their driver was negotiating the press of traffic at Marble Arch, a cheeky urchin shouted from the curb, "You don't 'alf look a treat, Red!" Delighted, Annie waved and smiled, bringing an icy reprimand from Aunt Agatha down on her head.

"Probably thought you were a streetwalker." Across the barrier of Miss Winter's upholstered bosom, Marigold tittered.

"Well, you can always judge someone by the company she keeps," Annie flashed back.

"Girls! Girls!" admonished Aunt Agatha. "Mind your manners. Marigold, you are not to refer to such a class of persons again. A true lady does not know that such people exist. And, Annie, you are too bold and forward in your ways."

The rest of the journey towards the

Trevelyns' house in Kensington was accomplished in stony silence.

It was a very large white house, quite modern, and set a little apart from its neighbors. A striped canopy was over the door and a red carpet stretched across the pavement where two constables stood on duty.

Annie had long cherished a dream of *descending* into a ballroom. But she was to find that most ballrooms were *up* or *through* rather than down.

They powdered their noses and left their cloaks in a room off the hall, then mounted the staircase to be greeted by their hosts, Lord and Lady Trevelyn. Aunt Agatha went first, then Marigold, and then Annie behind her sister. They had almost reached the top of the stairs when Marigold jerked her elbow backward and caught Annie full in the middle.

Annie lost her balance and fell backward. She would have toppled down the length of the stairs to the tiled hall below had she not cannoned into the man who was mounting the staircase directly behind her.

He caught her in his arms and steadied her on the stair, then smiled down at her.

She had a bewildering mixture of sensations, sights, and emotions.

There was the feel of a hard, muscled arm

around her waist; a masculine smell of cologne and tobacco. A startled glance upward revealed a handsome, tanned face with sleepy blue eyes fringed by long lashes, a mobile, humorous mouth, and a strong chin.

And then he spoke. "Well, it's my lucky evening after all. Life is stale, flat, and unprofitable, I thought, and this ball is going to fortify my jaded opinion, and then all of a sudden a beautiful redhead is thrown into my arms."

"I wasn't thrown," said Annie, breathlessly disengaging herself. "I was pushed."

"Really! By whom?"

Annie looked up. People were passing them on the stairs, casting them amused glances. Of Marigold and Aunt Agatha, there was no sign.

"Oh, never mind," said Annie. "Thank you for saving me."

"Where is your chaperone?"

"I think she's forgotten about me or she thinks I am following behind," Annie replied. "That is, my aunt is my chaperone. She must have gone ahead into the ballroom with Marigold."

"And which one of 'em pushed you?"

"Oh, I must just have tripped," said Annie hurriedly. It would be too vulgar for words to start accusing her sister to this sleepy, smiling gentleman.

"Then I shall escort you," he said, holding out his arm.

Annie cast a fleeting look up at his handsome face as she once again mounted the stairs. It was a pity he didn't have more animation, she decided.

Lady Trevelyn, a tall, arrogant lady with a high nose and high color, extended a limp hand to the curtsying Annie and then murmured to Annie's companion, "Delighted to see you, Jasper."

"Jasper." Annie giggled. "You sound like a story-book villain."

"Oh, I am." He smiled lazily. "I'm quite awfully wicked. Now what is your name? The majordomo is waiting.

Annie murmured her name.

The majordomo shouted, "The Marquess of Torrance, Lady Anne Sinclair."

Annie turned to her companion to say "So *you're* the Marquess of Torrance," but he was already bowing and turning to make his way to join a party of friends.

Aunt Agatha sailed up, looking pleased with Annie for the first time. "I didn't know you knew Torrance."

"I didn't. I mean, I don't. Marigold pushed

35

me down the stairs and I fell against him."

Aunt Agatha sighed. "When will you stop this childish behaviour of blaming Marigold for everything? No, not another word."

Annie joined Marigold, who was sitting on a rout-seat against the wall, pouting.

"How *bold* you are, Annie, to pretend to stumble so that you could get an introduction. But it doesn't work. Anyone could see that he wasn't in the least interested in you."

"You shouldn't be so nasty," retorted Annie. "It makes your face go all funny."

That struck home. Marigold switched on a glowing smile.

Annie thought furiously. Now that she knew that the man who had saved her from falling was none other than the Marquess of Torrance, he was all at once imbued with a sudden charm.

Annie still had a great deal of the schoolgirl in her. She had also been brought up to believe that any gently bred woman's sole goal in life was to secure a husband, the way a man might wish to succeed in, say, an army career. And so ambition and competition were born anew. She would like to show Marigold that she, Annie, could secure a husband. She would also like to get the one man her sister seemed interested in.

Her large gray eyes roamed around the ballroom. It was not as large as she expected it to be, but it was a very elegant room for all that. An orchestra played the inevitable "Merry Widow" waltz from behind a screen of palms and hothouse flowers. The smells of exotic cooking wafted in from the supper room. The men were beginning to sign their names in the girls' dance cards, and a few couples were circulating the floor.

And then, all at once, she saw the now familiar figure of the Marquess of Torrance studying herself and Marigold. She would not have recognised him from the photograph. In the photograph he had looked vital and alert. In reality he was even more handsome, but he seemed languid and sleepy.

His clothes were exquisitely tailored, and he wore a fine set of diamond studs in his shirt. He drew on a pair of white gloves and began to stroll in her direction.

Annie's heart beat hard.

And then he bent his black head over Marigold's hand and asked her for the next dance. He smiled lazily down at Annie, then turned and murmured something polite to Aunt Agatha, who was sitting on Marigold's other side. Then he led Marigold onto the floor.

Marigold turned and flashed a triumphant smile at Annie. All of Annie's newfound confidence in her appearance deserted her. It never dawned on her that the marquess would naturally ask the elder sister first. She felt that no one at all would ask her to dance.

And so she was quite startled to find a young man with a large, waxed moustache looking down anxiously at her and waiting to sign her card.

Annie danced very well. As the evening wore on, although her card was rapidly being filled up, her triumph had a sour taste, for the marquess showed no signs of asking her to dance.

At last, there was only one space left, the last waltz. Just when she had given up hope, he seemed to materialize beside her. "If you are not too frightened to dance with such a wicked man as myself, Lady Annie, then may I beg the pleasure of the last dance?"

Annie mutely nodded, and he wrote his name in the last space on her card. "Annie" was all she could think of. Not "Anne." Marigold must have said something, must have told him she was called Annie.

Anticipation of that last dance quite removed Annie from reality. She was sure she chatted with her partners; she vaguely remembered that a Mr. Russell had taken her in to supper and that he had talked about hunting with religious fervor. Soon the last dance loomed up, and there was no sign of the marquess. Had he forgotten? Inside her white silk ball gloves, Annie's hands began to feel damp with nervous perspiration.

He had not danced with Marigold again, that was one consolation. But then he had danced with so very few ladies.

And then all at once it was time for the last waltz and he was walking towards her, mysteriously appearing from somewhere.

Her heart beat hard. She was not in love with him, of course, but ambition can be almost as burning and heady an emotion as love.

Lady Trevelyn did not believe that very slow, romantic waltzes should be featured at the end of the evening. They could lead to quite impossible alliances. And so this waltz seemed to be played in double-quick time.

The Marquess of Torrance did not pay any attention to the beat, merely moving slowly round and around, and holding Annie rather more tightly at the waist than he should.

Annie also found that she was being danced slowly into one corner while the rest of the guests spun around the area of the floor.

"Why are we staying here?" she asked. "It looks odd."

"I haven't the energy, my dear Lady Annie," said the marquess. "Terribly fatiguing to go hopping about the place at this hour in the morning. I don't approve. Besides, my face gets all red and my shirt wilts, and you wouldn't want that to happen."

"But I feel a bit silly. If feel as if everyone is looking at us," ventured Annie timidly.

"They are?" He stopped suddenly, stared about him with a hard expression, and then relaxed. "No," he said equably. "No one is paying us the least attention."

He must be blind, thought Annie. Marigold's glare is stabbing me from straight across the floor.

"You know," he went on seriously as he put his arm firmly around her waist again, "you really must stop thinking that everyone is looking at you. That sort of thing can lead to all sorts of trouble. There's a friend of mine, Bertie, *he* thought that. Drove him mad. He solved the problem all the same."

"What did he do?"

"He shaved all of his hair off. Bald as a coot. Didn't wear a hat. Of course, everyone looked at him then. Everyone *does* stare at a bald chap when he's quite young. Never wore a hat, did

Bertie. He also wore his coat back to front. It was a great relief, he said, to know that everyone *was* actually staring at him."

Annie stifled a giggle. "Is he still bald?"

"Oh, no," said the marquess, seriously. "He was quite cured. After a month of walking around like an eccentric billiard ball, he felt he'd had it, so he put his coat on the right way and grew his hair again."

"I simply don't believe you."

"Now that's very rude," chided the marquess. "How can we possibly become friends if you are going to disbelieve every word I say?"

"Friends?" said Annie. "I – I mean . . . you . . . me?"

"Why not? It has been known to happen. It's not very shocking, you know. I mean, people aren't going to whisper behind their gloves and say, 'Isn't it *shocking*? Torrance is *friends* with Lady Annie,' now are they?"

"Well . . . no. You're teasing me!"

"I? Nonsense. I am too lazy to tease anyone."

"The music has stopped and we're still dancing and people *are* looking at us!"

"So they are," agreed the marquess, coming to an abrupt halt and gazing about the room with a ludicrous expression of dismay on his face. "I was enjoying your company so much, Lady Annie. I quite forgot. Well, I shall probably call on you tomorrow. Manchester Square, I think your sister said. I'd better ask Miss Winter's permission. What a lot of white stuff that lady does put on her front. Old Colonel Butterworth danced with her last season, you know, and his valet had to use a bucket of turpentine on his evening clothes to repair the damage. The old boy smelled of turpentine for the rest of the Season, and that sort of thing's not fair, not when you can't afford another suit of togs. I wonder if Miss Winter has ever considered that? Perhaps I shall tell her."

"No!" said Annie, in alarm.

But he was already ambling indolently in Aunt Agatha's direction. She watched him anxiously, but he was obviously not saying anything shocking.

"I think you girls did very nicely," commented Aunt Agatha, on the way home. "Torrance asked for permission to call."

"Yes, to see me," said Marigold triumphantly.

"Well, he didn't say *just* you, Marigold. He asked for permission to call on *both* of you."

Marigold gave a jarring laugh. "Annie!

42

When was anyone ever interested in her, with me around?"

"We've never had young men around before," Annie flashed back.

"Young! Pooh! Torrance is at least thirty."

"That's not old, but maybe it's too old for *you*?"

"Oh, no," Marigold said sweetly. "I have quite made up my mind to break his heart."

"It's me he's interested in," said Annie defiantly. "He asked *me* for the last waltz."

"And what a little fool you looked, too, dancing on after the music had stopped. Lord Clabber, who had been dancing with me, just laughed and said you must have had a little too much to drink at supper."

Annie's face flamed with mortification. "Well, it wasn't my fault. It was *Torrance* who didn't want to stop dancing. And he – he said we were *friends*, so there."

"Oh, really! Just like a big brother. Now men in love never want to be friends. Wicked marquess! To cultivate the friendship of my little sister just to get close to me."

"That's it!" exclaimed Annie, seeing that Aunt Agatha had fallen asleep. "I'm going to punch you on the nose!"

She sprang to her feet and the open landau swayed dangerously. "Just you try!" screamed

43

Marigold, lashing out with her fan.

"Ladies! Ladies!" called the coachman. "Your ladyships will have us over."

"What is going on here?" Aunt Agatha's stern tone as she woke up made both girls subside silently into their seats. "Can't I close my eyes for a moment, Annie, without you starting a fight?"

The dawn sky was pearl gray and the birds were beginning to sing in the trees of Hyde Park as the horses pulling the landau clopped over the cobblestones. A water cart was washing the street silver, and already shopkeepers were taking the shutters down from their windows. A crossing sweep doffed his hat, and Annie, despite her sulks, could not resist giving him a wave. Her anger never lasted long.

Carts laden with flowers and vegetables were straining toward Covent Garden market. Thin spirals of smoke were beginning to rise from the chimneys, and, in Manchester Square, there was the smell of frying bacon as the servants started the day's work.

The footmen jumped down from the back-strap to assist the ladies in alighting. When they were on the shallow steps in front of the house, Annie suddenly remembered Marigold's wicked push at the ball. As her sister moved forward to enter the house, she stuck out her foot. Marigold tripped and went sprawling into the hall.

With a scream of rage, Marigold leaped to her feet, her fingernails ready to rake Annie's face. Then she saw the look on Aunt Agatha's face and subsided into noisy sobs, burying her dry eyes in a wisp of a handkerchief.

"Go to your room, Annie," said Miss Winter, in awful tones. "I will need to think of a way to punish you. If this behaviour continues, I shall have no alternative but to send you home."

"Mother locks her in her room when she's bad," said Marigold.

"Then that is what I shall do," said Aunt Agatha. "Go, Annie, and I shall come with you and turn the key in the door and take it away. You will not leave your room until you have written, five hundred times, 'A lady does not betray excess of emotion,' and you will spend at least the whole of tomorrow locked up."

"But the Marquess of Torrance is coming to call," wailed Annie. "It's not fair. Why am I always the one who's punished when *she* . . ."

"That's enough!" Aunt Agatha pushed Annie toward the stairs with surprising strength.

Annie realized that it would be useless to protest. As she mounted the stairs, she could not resist looking back.

Lady Marigold Sinclair stuck out her tongue.

Chapter Three

ANNIE awoke to a feeling of doom. A housemaid was pulling back the curtains to flood the bedroom with sunlight. Then the maid went out quickly and locked the door behind her.

Annie blushed all over with mortification. Being punished at home where the servants were part of the family was one thing. Being punished the very day after you've put your hair up for the first time, and in front of strange London servants, too, was quite awful. She lay in bed, staring at the ceiling, and thirsted for revenge.

As the morning wore on, despite the fact that Annie had only had a few hours' sleep, she found it impossible to rest. At least it appeared that she was not to be subjected to the bread-and-water treatment. A surprisingly tasty luncheon was delivered to her. Annie did not know that by now the servants all detested Marigold, who bullied them in a way she would not have dared to do at home.

Sheets of paper were laid out on a little writing desk so that she could write her "lines." She wrote that a lady did not betray excess of emotion fifty times and then, with a sigh, put down her pen. The room was becoming uncomfortably hot, so she went to open the window and then leaned out. All those free people strolling about below her! She wondered what Marigold was doing. At least there had been no sign of the marquess.

Her red hair tumbled about her face in a riot of soft curls, all that was left of her elaborate coiffure after she had brushed it out. She was wearing a tailored alpaca skirt and a pin-striped blouse with a stiff little collar.

She was twisting this way and that way in front of the glass, pushing up her hair to see how it would look in a different style, when she heard the rattle of a carriage on the cobblestones outside.

The carriage stopped.

Annie rushed to the window.

The Marquess of Torrance was descending from his chariot – always to be pronounced "char-ot" since no lady ever used all of the syllables. He was carrying his hat in his hand

and the sun shone on his crisp black hair. His beautifully tailored, dove-gray coat fell open to reveal an ornately embroidered waistcoat. He had arrived in an open carriage and that meant that, had Annie been at liberty to go for a drive, she would not have needed a chaperone. But she could not go. There was no way. Her bedroom was three floors above the street and the door was firmly locked.

Downstairs, the Marquess of Torrance smiled blandly on Aunt Agatha and Lady Marigold. He had not asked for Annie.

Now Marigold was firmly convinced that the way to entrap a man was to drive him mad with rejection. She knew she was looking extremely pretty in a pale pink, flowered silk skirt and a blond lace blouse with a high, boned collar.

So when the marquess said gently that it was a beautiful day for a drive in the park, Marigold tossed her head, and, with what she hoped was a killing laugh, said, "Is it, my lord? I declare I hadn't noticed."

"I thought all ladies enjoyed showing off their fashions in the park," said the marquess.

"For myself," said Marigold, who had not, as yet, been for a drive in the park at the fashionable hour, "I cannot see the fascination in simply going around and around in a carriage."

Aunt Agatha glared at Marigold, but Marigold sat with a serene smile on her face. The marquess, she knew, would promptly beg for her company, and, after a certain amount of pretty hesitation, she would finally allow him the honor.

He was sitting, very much at his ease, in an armchair that faced the window. "In that case," he said, "I will not press you to do something that you obviously despise, Lady Marigold. I shall try my luck with your sister and hope that she will take pity on me."

"I am afraid Lady Annie is indisposed," began Aunt Agatha, "and you must forgive Marigold's naughty teasing, my lord, for . . ."

"Oh, do not trouble to apologize," said the marquess. "Unless I am much mistaken, Lady Annie has fully recovered and is shortly about to join us."

"Why, what do you mean? Annie is . . ."

"Just outside the window," said the marquess blandly.

Aunt Agatha and Marigold were sitting in chairs facing him, with their backs to the window. They turned slowly around, and Aunt Agatha let out a shrill scream.

A pair of white, glacé kid, button boots were

dangling outside the window somewhere at the top of the frame. Inch by inch, the apparition descended. First the boots, then an inch of frilly petticoat, then a white tussore skirt, then a jade-green silk blouse, and then Annie's red head topped with a wickedly simple straw hat.

"She's gone mad," said Marigold shrilly, as Annie's gloved hands holding on to a rope of sheets cautiously descended.

Miss Winters closed her mouth and leaped into action. "John!" she shouted to the footman. "Rescue Lady Annie immediately. Dear me! She will be quite killed."

"I wonder how one gets quite killed?" asked the marquess, but the ladies were not paying any attention.

Annie was now adding insult to injury by placing the soles of her boots against the window so that she could swing out over the area railings in front of the house and land on the pavement.

The footman caught her just as she showed every sign of swinging back like a pendulum through the window glass.

Marigold and Aunt Agatha sat down again, their backs rigid. The door opened and Annie sailed in. Marigold waited triumphantly for her sister's humiliation in front of the marquess. Annie looked disgustingly band-box fresh considering her perilous escape from her room. Marigold felt that Annie had come off the best at the hands of the dressmaker by not having her clothes chosen for her by Aunt Agatha.

Annie curtsied to the marquess, who had risen to his feet.

"My apologies, my lord," she said lightly, bestowing a charming smile on her aunt. "I'm afraid the silly servants locked me in my room by mistake."

"Then you were most enterprising to escape from it," he said smoothly, with a smile lurking in his eyes. He was well aware that Annie had been locked up for some misdemeanor. For if she had been locked in by accident, she had only to shout or ring for the servants.

"I see you are ready to join me for a drive, Lady Annie," he went on, "and since your sister does not favor the exercise, I fear you will have to put up with my company. With your permission, of course, Miss Winters."

Annie looked pleadingly at her aunt. Marigold gleefully waited for the storm to break.

Aunt Agatha said mildly, "Of course you are free to go, Annie. I know his lordship to be a fine whip, so you will be in good hands."

Marigold made a gulping, spluttering noise.

When Annie and the marquess had left the room, Marigold started to scream, "How could you? How dare she? I shall write to Mother . . . *Oh! Oh! Oh!*"

"Shut up!" said Aunt Agatha. "Yes, it might do very well," she went on slowly. "Torrance may be a rake, but he's quite a catch. I must telephone Mrs. Burlington and tell her the news. She has been after him for *years* for one of those pasty faced daughters of hers and she said only the other night that, as an *unmarried* lady, I would find it a disadvantage in getting you girls fixed up. Hah! Wait until she hears *this*!"

She sailed from the room, leaving Marigold to writhe on the floor in quite the worst fit of hysterical rage that that young lady had ever had.

Annie was too unsophisticated to realize that Miss Winter had some grounds for being so triumphant. The Marquess of Torrance had never at any time in his life shown enough interest in any young debutante to take her driving. He had kept a succession of demimondaine ladies, which was not to be held against him. Such behaviour in a marquess was glamorous. In Mr. Joe Bloggs of Clapham, say, it would be considered disgusting and immoral.

Now that she had achieved the beginnings of her ambition, Annie felt quite shy and tongue-tied as she sat beside Torrance in the carriage. He was handling his pair of matched bays himself, and there was only one groom on the backstrap. The open carriage was well-sprung and bowled along with a gentle, swaying motion.

The sun sparkled on varnish and metal. "It's – it's a very nice carriage," said Annie, at last.

"Yes, isn't it," he replied equably. "It's a mobile map of the world in its way. The framework is made of English ash, the panels are Honduras mahogany, the footboards are American ash, the shafts are Jamaican lance-wood, the wheels are Canadian hickory, and the spokes are English oak. There! I have furthered your education."

"Yes," said Annie, who could not think of anything else to say.

She slid a sideways glance at him under the shadow of her hat. He had a strong face in profile, and his long hands holding the reins seemed strong also, despite their whiteness and manicured nails.

But everything about him was too studied, too mannered. She wondered suddenly if he really cared very strongly about anything except his clothes and his horses.

"Would you like a motorcar?" he asked.

"Oh, that's just a fad, or so Papa says."

"I would. I'm thinking of buying one."

"But what would you do with your horses?"

"Use them as well, for pleasant outings like this. Use the motorcar when I have to go to the country."

"I can't imagine anyone loving one of those contraptions the way they love their horses."

"Oh, but they do, I assure you. In some cases, more so. Take my friend Jeffrey Withers. Now he bought a Lanchester only last year and he's had endless trouble with it. It always seems to be breaking down. But he loves it. Although he doesn't think of it as an 'it,' if you take my meaning. He thinks of it as 'she', just like boats. He calls his motorcar Bessie and he talks to it day and night.

"I passed him once on the Brighton road and he was cranking the engine like mad and saying, 'Come along, Bessie, I know you can do it. Jeffrey loves you. Just give a little cough for old Jeffrey to show you're alive.' "

"You either have strange friends or you are teasing me," said Annie. "First you tell me about someone who shaved his head bald . . ."

"Bertie."

"Yes, Bertie. And now there's this Jeffrey who talks to his motorcar."

"Never mind. Here we are. London at play."

Annie studied the other carriages and their occupants with great interest as they drove around by the Serpentine.

Some of the women drove themselves. Annie twisted around to admire a pretty little blonde in a plethora of pink ruffles and pink maribou who was handling her whip like an expert. As she watched, the blonde looked fully at the marquess, gave him a saucy smile and the merest flicker of a wink, and then she trotted sedately past, the little parasol on the end of her whip, also pink to match the rest of her outfit.

"That pretty lady winked at you," said Annie.

"She did? I'm flattered," said her companion. "Now what is the name of that tree over there? I never can remember it."

"Ladies don't wink," said Annie, beginning to feel cross although she could not understand why. Perhaps it was because the blonde had reminded her of Marigold.

"Elder, surely."

"Than whom?"

"Not that elder. I mean, the name of

the tree."

"I don't know," said Annie, thinking furiously. Good manners meant that she could not pursue any subject that her companion wanted to drop.

Vague social rumors and bits of gossip began to drift through her head. About the Marquess of Torrance being a wild, young man-about-town. Of course he wasn't young, but it seemed that all bachelors were young until they reached their dotage.

The blonde in the pink dress had been very pretty, very pretty indeed. But not a lady. Ladies did not wink, thought Annie, folding her soft mouth into a prim line.

"Have you indigestion, or have I said something to offend you?"

She realised with a start that her companion had been studying her face. "No," she said. "No, my lord, I was thinking of something . . . well, something else."

"And not me? Ah, well . . . there is Lady Trevelyn . . ." Annie bowed. "And there is Mrs. Wayling, a friend of my mother." Annie bowed again.

"I somehow did not think of you as having a mother," she said, as a chilly little breeze sprang up and a passing cloud cast its shadow over the waters of the Serpentine.

"You mean you thought I sprang fully armed in a natty gent's suit from my father's head, or something like that?"

"No. I mean, one does not think of older people having mothers."

"Ouch!"

"I mean, not that you are old, just mature," pleaded Annie.

"Well-seasoned like the English oak?"

"Not quite, my lord. I meant . . . Oh, it's too hard to explain. Is your mother in town?"

"No, she and my father are in the country."

"Yes, of course. Your father is the Duke of Dunster. Marigold and I looked you up in Debrett."

"How thorough of you. Now, tell me how it came about that you were escaping from your room in that dramatic manner?"

"I told you. It was the servants. They locked me in by mistake."

"So you did . . . tell me, I mean."

"You don't believe me?"

"What on earth gave you that idea, Lady Annie? I believe everything you say."

Annie bit her lip. They were rolling toward the gates of Hyde Park again. She felt that she somehow *had* to get him to say something intimate. Something she could throw in Marigold's face.

The day was clouding up, and she shivered slightly in the rising dusty wind.

They stopped in the press of traffic at Hyde Park Corner, and he reached behind her, pulled up a mohair carriage rug, and gently wrapped it about her shoulders. His face was suddenly very close to her own, so she could see the lazy smile on his mouth and the thick eyelashes veiling his eyes.

"Now you should feel warmer." His voice held a caressing note.

"Thank you," whispered Annie, feeling gauche and schoolgirlish. Marigold would have said something flirtatious and made the most of the moment. But, all at once, the traffic moved and he took up the reins again.

"Shall you be at the Worthingtons' ball tonight?" he asked.

"I don't think so," said Annie. "My aunt said nothing about what we were to do this evening."

"Oh, I think you'll find you're invited," he said easily. "Everyone's going to be there."

Annie remembered all the gilt-edged invitation cards stuck in the corner of the looking glass in the drawing room. She had not studied them, knowing the names would mean nothing to her. She had another ball gown that should have arrived that morning. It was the same leaf green as her blouse and would turn Marigold's eyes the same color with envy.

"The Worthingtons are very grand," he was saying. "Not only are we to have a ball but a fireworks display as well."

"I hope we're invited," said Annie anxiously. "I've never seen a fireworks display."

"What! Not even on Guy Fawkes Night?"

"We don't celebrate Guy Fawkes in Scotland."

"No November fifth! What a heathen country. Ah, here we are." He called to his groom, who ran round and held the horses while the marquess escorted Annie to the door.

"Thank you for a very pleasant drive, my lord," said Annie shyly.

"My pleasure." He bent and kissed her gloved hand, smiling into her eyes in a way that left her feeling strangely breathless. Then he turned and climbed back into his carriage, cracked his whip, and moved off as Miss Winter's butler opened the door.

Annie trailed into the drawing room, unpinning her hat as she did so and feeling strangely flat.

Aunt Agatha came sailing in, looking flustered. "My dear Annie, I have just had a telephone call from your papa, and such news!

It appears that Crammarth's second cousin, the disgraceful one that went to America, had died – he was older than your papa, so one must *not* mourn – and he has left your papa a vast fortune. Just think! Marigold is a wealthy, wealthy heiress. You, too, my dear. But, of course, Marigold's child will be the heir because, naturally, she will marry first."

"I might well marry before Marigold," said Annie.

"Oh, my dear, you are pinning your hopes on the wicked Jasper. Well, I am afraid we were all a bit silly about that. I telephoned that horrid Mrs. Burlington to tell her that Torrance was quite smitten with you, for it seemed as if he must be since he never entertains debutantes, and she said that Torrance had said at the Trevelyns' ball that you were 'an amusing little thing.' Now, I ask you, is that what a man with any serious intentions would say about a girl? And, of course, with a beauty like Marigold around, it's amazing that he noticed you *at all*.

"I didn't believe her, and said so, but Mrs. Burlington said that Torrance had said that to Bertie Ffrench, so I telephoned Bertie Ffrench. He was maddeningly vague but said, 'Oh, you mean the gel with the hair like a pillar box? Jasper did say something fatherly.'

So there! You will just need to look around for someone more your weight. I have not forgotten your punishment, so you may finish your lines while I escort Marigold to the Worthingtons'."

"Why can't I go to the Worthingtons'?" asked Annie, in a bewildered voice. Her emotions were going up and down like a see-saw. There was so much to assimilate. Papa was very rich, which meant that she, as well as Marigold, must now be considered an heiress. The marquess had said that she was merely an "amusing little thing." And she was not to go to the Worthingtons'.

"Well, you see," said Aunt Agatha, "it was a teensy bit foolish on my part. I was so concerned with finding a husband for Marigold that when Mrs. Worthington told me about the ball, well, I only mentioned Marigold, and it would be too pushing to take you along because it would upset the supper arrangement to have one more, and the Worthingtons are such sticklers. So you see. And you are being punished anyway."

"It's just *not* fair," said Annie, rebelliously.

"On the contrary, it is very fair. Despite your appalling behavior, I allowed you the treat of a drive with Torrance, so you have had quite enough for one day. Now go to your room and don't let me hear another word!"

When Annie reached her room, she turned the key in the door. Marigold would no doubt be calling shortly to crow over her defeated sister.

Annie paced up and down, up and down. In her mind's eye, someone, not necessarily the marquess, would propose to Marigold at the Worthingtons', and she would have to take second place again as she had done all of her young life.

Annie's very dull and sheltered upbringing had kept her very emotionally immature. First a nanny, and then a governess, who favored Marigold no matter what she did, had made her very bitter toward her sister. She burned with hurt and a desire for revenge. Somehow, she just *had* to get to that ball.

The door handle turned, then stopped. "Let me in!" called Marigold.

"Go away," said Annie, furiously.

"Oh, you silly cat. You're just mad because I'm going and you're not."

Annie took a deep breath, then said loudly and clearly, "Of course I am furious. I had hoped to be allowed to spend some time with my fiancé."

"What!"

"You heard me."

"You can't mean Torrance. Oh, it's too stupid. You're such a liar. I'm going to tell Auntie."

Marigold's footsteps could be heard retreating rapidly down the corridor. Annie slowly went over and unlocked the door. She had just told one terrible lie. And, somehow, she knew all at once that she was going to go on telling it.

Aunt Agatha opened the door and walked into the room. "Now, what's all this tarradiddle, Annie?"

"Send her away first," said Annie grimly, pointing to Marigold, who was hovering in the doorway.

"Oh, very well, but if this is another of your . . . Go away, Marigold. Now, Annie!"

"Well, he did propose to me," said Annie defiantly. "I didn't tell you because he said he would be writing to Papa and that he would be calling to see you tomorrow."

Aunt Agatha sank into a chair and stared at Annie with a bewildered look on her face. "One would almost think you were telling the truth," she said slowly.

"I am," said Annie, "and if you don't believe me, well, there's an easy way to find out."

"Which is . . .?"

"Why, telephone him," said Annie, sending up a silent prayer that her aunt would react as she expected her to.

"No. I couldn't possibly do that. It would be questioning his honor. If you are lying, then it would make a terrible fool of me. And if you are not, then he would think me extremely rude."

"In that case," said Annie, trying to keep her voice level, "do you not think that the best idea would be to take me with you to the Worthingtons'? Jasper said he was looking forward to dancing with me."

"Oh, very well. I shall telephone Mrs. Worthington and tell her to expect an extra guest. I shall say nothing to Torrance unless he chooses to speak to me. But if he ignores you, if his manner proves that he has not the slightest interest in you, then you will be sent home."

With that, Aunt Agatha left the room, leaving Annie in a misery of anxiety. To follow her aunt and apologize, to say that she had made the whole thing up, would mean that she would be sent back to Scotland anyway.

Even the sight of her new green ball gown spread out on the bed did nothing to allay her fears.

Marigold was nearly dancing about with glee before they got into the carriage that was to bear them to the Worthingtons'.

"Of all the awful lies," she whispered. "Won't it be fun seeing Torrance's face when I tell him."

"You won't," said Annie, hopefully. "Aunt will stop you."

"So it *is* a lie," hissed Marigold, as the steps to the carriage were let down.

"If you choose to think so, then that is your affair," retorted Annie, in what she hoped was a chilling voice.

"Please let him not be there," she prayed as the carriage bore them inexorably nearer to the Worthingtons'.

The Worthingtons lived in a large mansion in Princes Gate, so the drive, unfortunately for poor Annie, was very short.

Again the red carpet, the canopy, the police, the stairs, and the hostess. Again the gentlemen bowing and scribbling their names in her card. Again Mr. Russell with his moustache and sideburns begging her for the supper dance.

"I'm surprised you didn't try to keep a dance for your fiancé." Marigold tittered from behind her fan.

"I did," said Annie defiantly. "The last.

That's the one he asked me to keep."

("Please, oh *please*, don't let him come.")

Aunt Agatha leaned across Marigold and addressed Annie in a threatening whisper, "Mind, young lady. No engagement, and back to Scotland you go. Oh, I just *know* you're lying. Why did I ever listen to you? Why can't you be more like your sister?"

"Who wants to be like *her*?" muttered Annie, but Miss Winter mercifully did not hear, and Annie's partner approached to claim her for the first dance.

Of course, the marquess would have to arrive just as she was beginning to relax. Just as she was beginning to enjoy herself. Please let him not speak to Marigold or Auntie!

Then Annie stumbled and fell over her partner's feet. "I must go," she blurted. "I have to tell my aunt something important." For the marquess was heading straight for Aunt Agatha.

Annie managed to get there at the same time. Under the cover of her fan, she winked and grimaced at him desperately. He raised his eyebrows slightly but turned away from Annie and bowed over Aunt Agatha's hand.

"My dear Lord Torrance," said Aunt Agatha, with a grim edge to her voice. "I must thank you for entertaining Lady Annie this afternoon."

"Not at all. The pleasure was mine entirely," he murmured.

"I gather you had a very interesting conversation," pursued Aunt Agatha.

"Quite," said the marquess, at his most urbane.

Annie heaved a sigh of relief. Now if she could get him alone and ask him to help her out of this jam!

'Oh, no! Marigold.

That young lady came tripping up on the arm of her partner. Annie closed her eyes.

"Lord Torrance!" cried Marigold, all false innocence. "My congratulations! Our little Annie has achieved the first engagement of the Season. When is the wedding to be?"

There was a heavy silence. Annie closed her eyes tighter.

They flew open at the sound of the marquess's amused, lazy drawl. "Oh, I think in about a month's time. Neither Annie nor myself believe in long engagements."

He turned to Annie who, by this time, was chalk white, and took her hand in his.

"You are a naughty puss, Annie," he said playfully. "You are supposed to wait for your father's permission before you tell anyone. I shall call on you tomorrow, Miss Winter, to formally request *your* permission as a start."

"Delighted," said Aunt Agatha faintly.

"Now, Annie," said the marquess, giving her limp hand a little shake. "Let me see your dance card. Who has the supper dance? Russell. Ah, well, he will let me have it now that he knows I have prior claim. There you are, Russell. You must really let me have this dance, old chap. You see, Lady Annie is engaged to me. You shouldn't all stand with your mouths open like that. I had a friend who kept doing that and do you know what happened to him?" He smiled benignly at his stunned audience.

"Well, one day, a blooming great wasp flew right into his mouth and stung him right in the back of the throat, and he nearly choked to death. Come along, Annie. The music's started."

Annie placed her hand on his arm, and he walked off with her to the center of the floor.

Somewhere behind them, Marigold began to scream.

Chapter Four

AT first the Earl and Countess of Crammarth were worried about the shortness of their younger daughter's engagement. Such speed was open to misinterpretation. They had traveled to London as soon as they had heard the news.

But the fact that their daughter had hooked the catch of London society was not to be overlooked. The marquess was all that was reassuring. And so they agreed to the early wedding.

Perhaps Annie would have called the whole thing off if she had been left alone in her fiancé's company. Perhaps she would have realized the danger of getting married simply for revenge. But no sooner had he won her parents' approval than he had taken himself off to France "on business," promising to return only the day before the wedding.

Also, revenge on Marigold was terribly sweet. Now Annie was the fêted and petted one. And so she went headlong toward her marriage to a man she did not know in the slightest and had not even kissed.

Annie had been deprived of affection and attention for as long as she could remember. She luxuriated in it now; she basked in it.

Marigold did all she could to puncture Annie's balloon of happiness.

"He's a masher," said Marigold, triumphantly. "And there're a lot of rumors around that he's short of money, and it's well known that his father expects him to support himself. He must have jumped at the chance when you threw yourself at his head. It was all around the ball as soon as we arrived that we were heiresses. Aunt Agatha told Mrs. Worthington on the telephone when she rang her to say that you were coming, and Mrs. Worthington told everyone else. You poor, deluded little thing! Think of all the mistresses he's had!"

"I shall change all that," said Annie stubbornly.

"Rakes never change," said Marigold. "Everyone except you knows that."

But those sorts of remarks were all Annie expected from Marigold. A man settled down once he was married. No one could expect him to behave like a monk before then. All of her romances had been full of wild and savage heroes who had been tamed and brought to heel by the love of a pure and innocent girl. So it must be true.

The time until the marquess's return from France hurried past in a bewilderment of fittings and pinnings and shopping. Marigold went alone to balls and parties with Aunt Agatha. The Earl and Countess of Crammarth bustled about Annie as if they had just given birth to her.

And then the marquess returned. Annie had met his parents and had searched, without success, their austere, cold faces for some sign of their son's sunny insouciance. They seemed to neither approve nor disapprove of her.

Her fiancé arrived too late for the wedding rehearsal, so Annie's cousin, Jimmy Sinclair, had to stand in as groom. But nothing could dim Annie's flying spirits, her heady feeling of success. The Countess of Crammarth was so engrossed with the multiple arrangements for a society wedding that she failed to arrange for the couple to be left alone when the marquess called to see his fiancée. She also failed to give that little talk to her daughter about the intricacies of the marriage bed.

Annie was almost as innocent as the day she was born when she walked proudly up to the altar of St. George's, Hanover Square, on her father's arm.

Her slim figure in a dress of priceless old lace gave the lie to the gossips who had hinted that there must be a sinister reason – in the heraldic sense – for the rushed wedding.

Marigold as maid of honor looked a blonde vision. But this was Annie's day of triumph. She could see no farther ahead than this one splendid, glorious day.

She knew that she and Jasper were to spend the night at his town house and then to travel to Paris on their honeymoon, but she thought vaguely of it all as a sort of family holiday.

The wedding breakfast was held at the newly opened Ritz Hotel in Piccadilly since Aunt Agatha's house in Manchester Square was not nearly large enough to hold all of the guests.

Annie's highly colored fairy tale went on. She sat proudly at the head table beside her husband and responded prettily to all of the toasts. Proudly, she took the floor with him, her long train looped gracefully over her arm.

Breathlessly, she allowed a bevy of maids to assist her into her going-away clothes. Joyfully, she threw the wedding bouquet as far away from Marigold as possible. It was caught by their governess, Miss Higgins, who turned quite pink with delight.

And then . . . and then . . . they were in *his* carriage, going to *his* town house in St. James's Square.

And it was all over.

She had been revenged on Marigold for all

those years of humiliation. She had had her day of triumph.

'Now what?

There was a coachman on the box and two splendid footmen on the backstrap. Barton, the maid, had been assigned to her as her very own.

But soon the coach would stop and the coachman would take the gaily decorated carriage round to the mews. The footmen would help her down and open the doors, and then they, too, would go away. Barton would prepare her mistress for bed and then she would leave.

And Annie would be alone with her husband.

All at once it burst over her head, the folly of what she had done.

The wedding night!

What was she supposed to do? What would he do – to her?

He ushered her into a pleasant, book-lined room on the ground floor of his house. "It's all very masculine," he said. "But you can make any changes you want."

The room smelled of leather and tobacco. The evening had turned chilly and a fire had been lit in the grate. There were pictures of horses and rather dark landscapes in heavy, gilt frames ornamenting the walls. The furniture was a harmonious mixture of periods. There was a Boulle writing table in one corner, and in another a pretty little bureau bordered with crushed mica by Pierre Golle. There were window seats by Chippendale and four Louis XV armchairs. Electricity had not been installed yet and the soft glow of two large oil lamps illuminated the room.

"Well," said Annie brightly. "Here we are."

"Yes," he echoed. "Here we are. Do you wish anything to eat?"

"No," said Annie. "I think I ate enough at the – the . . . reception."

"In that case, my love . . ."

"But I would like something to drink."

"Very well." He touched the bell and then murmured something to the butler.

"Now, Annie," he said, walking toward her. Annie held on to the chair back for support.

"Your servants will – will . . . enter at any moment, Jas-Jasper, and we should not . . . I mean . . ."

"Quite," he said equably. "Why don't you sit down? You look as if you're about to face a firing squad. Or would you like to retire to your room and freshen up? Yes, why don't you do that, and I will have the champagne sent upstairs."

"Oh, thank you," said Annie, overwhelmed with relief. She never thought that he meant to join her.

Her new quarters were spacious and elegant, and showed all the signs of having been recently decorated. There was a sitting room and a bedroom, in feminine shades of rose.

The large wardrobe in the bedroom held only her dresses and coats, and the two chests of drawers were full with the rest of her trousseau, which had been brought round earlier in the day and unpacked by Barton.

Annie's fear slowly left her. There was no sign of any masculine occupation. These were her rooms. He obviously planned to sleep in a suite of his own.

The bed was pretty and very French-looking, with its white-painted cane back and canopy of white lace. It was also very large.

Annie sat by the fire in the sitting room – what luxury to have a fire in summer! – and turned over the weighty responsibilities of marriage in her mind. She would be expected to produce an heir, although she had not the slightest idea of how that was to be achieved. Then she must see the housekeeper when they returned from Paris and go over the books.

Her thoughts were interrupted by the opening of the door. Her husband entered carrying a tray with a bottle of champagne and two tall, thin crystal glasses.

Annie fought down the fears that were rising up in her again, telling herself that he *was* her husband and that it was natural he should join her in her sitting room.

He sat down opposite her and poured the champagne. Annie had already drunk quite a great deal of wine that day, what with all the toasts, but she realised that her mouth was dry and she was very thirsty indeed. She drained her glass in one gulp and held it out to be refilled.

"I'm nervous as well," said the marquess, in a gentle voice that she had never heard him use before. "I haven't been married before."

He then went on to talk about the wedding reception, who was who on his side of the family and what they did, interspersing all the facts with amusing anecdotes that were so ridiculous that Annie was sure they were fictitious.

Somehow, during all this, they had succeeded in not only drinking the one bottle of champagne but also another that he had rung for while he was talking.

Annie was not aware that she had drunk

most of it; she was only aware that she was feeling hazy and lazy and relaxed, and everything he said began to seem exquisitely funny.

And somehow it all seemed natural when he gently took her glass from her hand and said, "Bed."

He stood up, drawing her up with him, pulling her into his arms. He bent his head and kissed her full on the mouth for the first time, his mouth gently pressing and exploring, his long fingers cradling her face.

At first she stayed immobile, her mouth tightly closed under his own. But a delightful, warm sort of prickly feeling like goose flesh began to run over her skin, and the pleasurable feel of his mouth on hers made her part her lips and kiss him back, her arms winding about his neck.

He swept her off her feet and carried her easily through to the bedroom, laying her down on the bed, his nimble, experienced fingers beginning to work loose the intricate fastenings of her dress.

Had she not drunk so much, had she not felt so cold and lost when he stopped caressing her, then she would surely have felt shocked. But with each new caress, her body seemed to scream for more, and when at last she was naked and he drew away to remove his own clothes, she could hardly wait for him to take her in his arms again.

He covered one small, rounded, firm breast with his hand, and Annie groaned against his lips. His body was hard and muscled, surprisingly so in so languid and lazy a man. He seemed to have muscles in the most unexpected places, Annie thought in a lucid moment before she went down under another wave of passion.

He paused, propping himself up on one elbow and looking down into her face, his eyes very blue and searching. Annie dreamily thought that he had never looked as handsome. His crisp black hair framed his tanned face. His eyelids were curved, giving his face a look of amused mockery. His nose was straight. His mouth strong and beautifully shaped. The strong column of his neck rose from a broad, powerful chest.

One hand languorously stroked the length of her back, then firmly clasped itself round one of her firm, rounded buttocks.

"Will we have a baby?" whispered Annie.

"Oh, I should think so," he said tenderly. "Lots and lots of little Jaspers."

Suddenly, all of the champagne she had drunk seemed to mount to Annie's brain in a rush and she giggled tipsily. "I've just *got* to have a baby before Marigold. Imagine going through all this just to get revenge and then finding she somehow managed to get married and produce an heir to the Crammarth fortune before me."

As she looked into his face, she was reminded of the shadow of the cloud passing over the shining waters of the Serpentine on that first drive with him. It was almost as if he had *dressed* his face, had covered it in some way, so that all of the laughing tenderness was gone, leaving only the familiar, lazy mockery.

"Such a pity we can't have that honeymoon in Paris after all," he said,

"Why?" Annie's mind fought to rise above the mists of alcohol.

"Oh, I have things to do in town. And now, good night, Annie."

Numbly she lay and watched him swing his legs out of bed, rise, and get dressed.

"You had better pull the covers over you or you'll catch cold," he said.

He said, "If I do not see you at breakfast, use any of my carriages you wish."

He said, "There is money in the desk in my study. Take as much as you like and buy yourself something."

He said, "And why don't you call on

Marigold in case her jealousy has reached a low ebb."

And then the door closed behind him.

Annie fought with drunkenness, with sleep.

She had said something terribly, terribly wrong.

But, for the life of her, she couldn't remember what it was.

The Marchioness of Torrance walked gloomily down the little main street of Britlingsea followed by her maid, Barton, and wondered whether to send a postcard to her husband.

Nothing had gone right since that wedding night, and yet, in a way, nothing had changed. It seemed to Annie that she was still a child being directed about what she should do by adults, one of the adults now being her husband.

She had been instructed on how to write checks and had been given permission to draw as much money from the bank as she wanted. The house in St. James's Square was terrifyingly well run, and the servants seemed to be in no need of supervision. The marquess had shown no inclination to take his new bride to his country estate, Frileton House. He escorted her to a few social engagements and left her almost as soon as they entered the room. He had then driven her to his parents' estate in his new motorcar, and there he had left her. Annie had endured the torments of loneliness and boredom since the duke and duchess hardly ever entertained.

Annie's parents had gone back to Scotland. Marigold had never once called since Annie's marriage, which was the only blessing Annie could think of.

And then one day while Annie was languishing at her in-laws, a letter from Marigold arrived. It was short but far from sweet. It reminded Annie that it was more than likely that the marquess had married her for her money. It instructed her to please see the enclosed cutting.

The cutting was from a Paris newspaper. Annie's French was very good although she did not need all that much knowledge of the language to read the caption under the photograph. The picture showed Jasper strolling down a boulevard with a pretty, little blonde on his arm. Annie easily recognized her as the blonde who had winked at him in the park. The caption said coyly that the Marquess of T—, an English milord, who had only recently been married to a certain Lady A., was holidaying in Paris with that well-known

English beauty, Miss S.

Now Annie could hardly remember anything of her wedding night except those marvelous, heady caresses that had inexplicably ceased so suddenly.

So she burned with humiliation. How Marigold must be crowing!

Two days of crying and despair passed, and then Annie became very angry indeed. Slowly she began to plan what to do. She decided to follow her first instinct, which was to get as far away from her in-laws as possible. He would not find her meekly waiting for him if he decided to return.

She told the duke and duchess that she was leaving for London immediately and asked Barton to pack her bags. Annie did not plan to stay in London above a day. For London still held Marigold. Although the Season was over and Marigold had gained many admirers but no proposals that she wanted to accept, she had decided to stay on with Aunt Agatha rather than to follow society north to Scotland for the opening of the grouse season.

The marquess's butler had recommended the seaside resort of Britlingsea as being "most exclusive" when he learned that her ladyship wished to remove herself from town.

So that was how Annie had ended up at the

quiet seaside resort with only her maid for company.

Exclusive turned out to mean dull.

The inhabitants of Britlingsea frowned on such seaside diversions as Pierrot and Punch-and-Judy shows. The promenade at the front where all those London trippers could strut was not for them.

And so the tiny town was still very much as it had been in the days when it had been a fishing village. Long, narrow lanes of cottages led from the one main street down to a small, rocky beach. Large villas had sprouted up around the town and one Grand Hotel at the west end catered to rich holidaymakers. Annie had taken a suite at the Grand. Now she was trying to enjoy her newfound freedom, but she found life there just as boring as it had been with her in-laws.

The sun was very bright and hot, with a hot August wind raising the dust from the cobbles and setting the striped awnings of the shops flapping. Glimpses of choppy blue sea could be seen at the end of each narrow lane leading from the main street. Great bunches of black sand shoes hung outside the shops, along with shrimping nets, buckets, and spades. Racks of colored postcards revolved on their stands.

Then in the post-office window her eye was

caught by a poster announcing: "Are You Tired of Being a Slave to Men? Why Shouldn't Women Get the Vote? Come on Thursday, August 19, at 7:30 p.m. to the Masonic Hall and hear that great suffragette, Miss Mary Hammond, speak. One shilling. Tea and cakes."

Annie looked at it thoughtfully. Members of the Women's Social and Political Union, the suffragettes, were often featured in the newspapers. They had become increasingly militant. They had planted a bomb in the home of Lloyd George, the Liberal leader, blowing up almost half of the furniture. They had claimed that it had merely been a warning, and suffragette leader, Mrs. Pankhurst, had taken the blame and had been sentenced to three years' penal servitude. Another woman had thrown a steel spike through the window of Lloyd George's cab. It had just missed his eye and cut him on the cheek. They had been damned as "man-haters," even by avowed feminists like H. G. Wells, despite the fact that the leaders of the movement, if they were not happily married, at least carried no sexual resentment.

But Annie believed them to be man-haters because of all the adverse publicity the movement had received in the press, and it was that

that made her want to go to the meeting. It was already August nineteenth. She had nothing else to do after she had eaten her solitary dinner at the Grand Hotel.

And so it was that she found herself that evening sitting on a hard bench in a drafty Masonic Hall listening to a large, tweedy woman telling her and about fifteen other women that men's sole goal in life was to debase and humiliate women and to keep them enslaved. Miss Hammond did not belong to the Women's Social and Political Union. She had once but aimed to form a splinter group. She had a sort of Lysistrata plan in which the women of Britain would unite by stopping marriage, stopping any form of intimate relations with men, therefore stopping child bearing "until the men are brought to their knees."

All of which seemed a splendid idea to poor, hurt, childish, humiliated Annie. She would have been amazed to learn that the leaders of the WSPU considered Mary Hammond quite mad. Miss Hammond did not want equality; she wanted superiority.

She was, nonetheless, a forceful personality and held the attention of her small audience until a little, local woman on the front bench called out, "Wot! No more slap an' tickle, then?"

"No!" replied Miss Hammond, majestically. "And no cuddling or canoodling either!"

Everyone except Annie burst out laughing, and had it not been for the prospect of tea and cakes, which they had already paid a shilling for, most of the audience would have left.

Annie did not know that every woman in the place was well aware of who she was until the lecture was over and she found herself being my-ladyed right, left, and center.

The audience was more interested in the tea and cakes and the pretty marchioness than in the speaker. For Annie did not know the effect that smart clothes and a good lady's maid had wrought in her. By any standards she was now an extremely pretty young woman.

But one by one the audience left and Annie found herself alone with Miss Hammond, who had asked her to stay behind for a moment.

"My dear Lady Torrance," said Miss Hammond. "I was extremely flattered to find a young and beautiful member of the aristocracy taking an interest in my one-woman movement. It is only a one-woman movement at the moment, but I hope to swell the ranks, *swell the ranks*."

"I'm surprised everyone knew who I was," said Annie.

"The hotel issues a circular with the names of all its notable guests," said Miss Hammond. "And, of course, people point you out to each other. What brought you to hear me, Lady Torrance?"

"I hate men," said Annie savagely.

"Yes, but you will find sometimes that we have to use the pests," said Miss Hammond. "That is why I call my movement 'Superiority for Woman' – no *direct* attack, you see."

She was a large woman with pale eyes and a mouth full of large, strong teeth. Her iron-gray hair was swept back in a bun, and she wore a mannish tweed suit with a short skirt that showed her ankles. She wore a man's tie and a shirt with a shiny celluloid collar.

But like quite a lot of people who teeter on the borderline of quasipolitical insanity, she had a warm, engaging, maternal charm and a humorous way of putting things, which belied the fact she had no sense of humor at all.

"In fact," Miss Hammond went on, "I have been invited to take tea tomorrow afternoon with a Very Important Person. I do wish you would come with me, Lady Torrance. You would be most impressed. He is a famous man who plans to support my cause. But it's hush-hush. *Very*."

"Oh, please call me Annie."

"Annie, then. And you must call me Mary. I gather from your tone that your recent marriage is not a happy one."

But Annie would not discuss her husband. "Who is this V.I.P.?" she asked.

Miss Hammond looked about her in the manner of a stage villain and whispered, "Mr. Shaw-Bufford."

"What? The chancellor of the exchequer?"

"Shh! The same."

"I find it hard to believe . . ."

"Oh, I know. But wait until you meet him."

"Is his wife . . .?

"He is not married."

"Then I don't see . . ."

"You will. Only say you'll come."

"Very well," said Annie.

"Good! Splendid!" exclaimed Miss Hammond. "I shall call at your hotel for you at quarter to five tomorrow. The chancellor has a villa just outside the town."

When Annie returned to the hotel and had been made ready for bed by Barton, she sat in front of the open window, looking out at the sea and wondering whether she had suffered from temporary insanity. She, Annie, did not hate men. She wished she did. She wished she could remember her husband's kisses with revulsion.

But her whole treacherous body ached and burned for him.

Mary Hammond was nuts. Absolutely, definitely, and quite positively nuts. If the chancellor of the exchequer was anywhere, it was not in Britlingsea. Mr. Shaw-Bufford was reported in the papers to be a sort of eighteenth-century gentleman, cultured, austere, with a biting wit. He had hoped, it was said, to be chosen by his party to be prime minister, but they had chosen the fiery Scotsman, James Macleod, instead.

But one thing was sure. Mr. Shaw-Bufford was too grand and too ambitious a politician ever to be seen in the company of someone like Miss Hammond.

Now mature, sensible, and growing-up people who wish to get out of an engagement sent a letter of apology by hand, or telephone if they are lucky enough to have that wonder of science. But immature young people like Annie do the first thing that comes naturally, and so Annie decided simply to give Miss Hammond the slip. She would go out walking at four-thirty, thereby neatly avoiding that lady, and she would leave Barton to make her apologies.

And so at precisely four-thirty the next

afternoon, Annie tripped lightly down the red-carpeted steps of the Grand Hotel and across the palm-tree-studded expanse of the entrance lounge – and straight into the massive bulk of Miss Hammond, who was, it seemed, parked across the hotel entrance.

"So you are early just like me, Annie," said Miss Hammond. "I didn't tell Mr. Shaw-Bufford that you were coming. *That* is going to be our little surprise."

"Yes," said Annie, gloomily.

Mary Hammond had at least *looked* like a sensible woman in the meeting hall last night. But today she seemed quite eccentric. Despite the heat of the afternoon, she was still wearing the tweeds, tie, and celluloid collar. Furthermore, she had cropped her gray hair, causing Annie to wonder why this man-hater should do her best to try to look like one.

Annie still did not believe that she was to meet Mr. Shaw-Bufford. But after they had walked a little way out of the town, Miss Hammond stopped in front of an imposing villa and pushed open one of the wrought-iron gates.

The gentleman who answered the door was Mr. Shaw-Bufford in person. Annie had seen photographs of him in *The Illustrated London News*.

He was a tall, thin man of about forty-five, with a narrow, almost monkish face with deep-set eyes and thin mouth. His hair was silver.

"Why, Miss Hammond," he said in a dry, precise voice.

"Who have we here? I thought I had made it plain that . . ."

"Oh, but this is the Marchioness of Torrance!"

"Delighted to have the pleasure of entertaining you, Lady Torrance," said Mr. Shaw-Bufford. "Come in, come in. I shall ring for Hodder to fetch another cup. I thought tea in the garden on a day like this would be very pleasant. I wonder if I could beg you to go ahead to the garden, Lady Torrance, while I have a little private word with Miss Hammond?"

Annie nodded and walked in the direction of the garden, which she could see through the open French windows of a long room at the end of the hall.

There was a table under an oak tree on the lawn. Out on the blue, blue ocean, white-sailed yachts darted here and there. Little, fleecy clouds curled across the deep blue of the sky. It was pleasantly cool in the shade of the tree, with only the sound of the gentle breeze moving in the leaves above her head and the hum of bees from a clump of hollyhocks beside the French windows.

All at once she was glad she had come. Somehow she had at least managed to meet a distinguished politician like Mr. Shaw-Bufford. Miss Hammond could not be quite the madwoman she seemed or the chancellor would surely have nothing to do with her.

A butler appeared with a silver tray and began to set a magnificent silver teapot, cream jug, and hot-water pot on the table. He was rather an unnerving-looking man. His livery of cutaway coat and striped waistcoat seemed to be too small for his great bulk. He had sparse strands of hair carefully combed over the top of his head. His face looked as if it had been smashed up at one time and then badly rearranged.

He did not once look at Annie or make any polite remark that one would normally expect from a butler. He disappeared and, after a few moments, reappeared with a large tray bearing plates of cucumber and salmon sandwiches, a magnificent plum cake, and a plate of hot scones oozing with butter.

Annie waited and waited after he had left. She was thirsty but did not want to pour herself a cup of tea until her host and Miss Hammond arrived.

The minutes began to drag by. A wasp hovered over the strawberry jam and she impatiently shooed it away.

Annie found herself wondering what it would be like to shed a few of her underclothes. She could feel the heat emanating from the horsehair pads on her hips and bust, the long Empire corset, and the layers of petticoats. The high, boned collar of her blouse was digging painfully into the back of her neck. Would they never come?

Just as she had given up and was reaching for the teapot, Mr. Shaw-Bufford and Miss Hammond appeared through the French windows. Miss Hammond looked . . . well, *strange*. Sort of elated and frightened and defiant and furtive – all at once.

"My apologies, your ladyship," said Mr. Shaw-Bufford. "I fear we have kept you waiting. Miss Hammond, will you pour for us? I hope to hear your husband speak in the Lords when the House sits again, Lady Torrance."

"I never thought of him even attending the House of Lords," said Annie, startled.

"He is a powerful speaker and a great loss to the House of Commons. Were he not a titled man, then I would certainly persuade him to try to run for office."

"I have not been married long," said Annie. "My husband is in France at the moment." She gave a very brittle, little laugh. "I don't know much about him at all."

That was surely the cue for Miss Hammond to expound her down-with-men philosophy, but she remained strangely silent. In fact the rest of the conversation did not touch on Miss Hammond's interest at all. At one point Annie tried to turn the conversation in that direction, feeling that it was only polite to do so, but Miss Hammond only seemed to want to talk about commonplaces, just like an ordinary housewife.

As it was, Annie had only eaten one sandwich and drunk one cup of tea when a look flashed between Miss Hammond and the chancellor, and, as if one cue, both rose to their feet at once.

"We really must be rushing along," said Miss Hammond. "The chancellor has a great deal of important papers to sign."

"Of course," murmured Annie. "I am sorry our meeting was so brief, Mr. Shaw-Bufford."

"And I, too. Will you be staying in Britlingsea long?"

All at once, Annie made the first grown-up decision of her life. She would return to London tomorrow. She would wait in town for her husband. And she would ask him why he had married her.

"I shall be leaving tomorrow," she said firmly. "On the early train."

"Splendid," he said. "I have a compartment reserved on the London train and would deem it an honor if you would share it with me, Lady Torrance."

"Thank you. Miss Hammond – I mean, Mary – will you be coming, too?"

Was Miss Hammond about to accept? Or did the sudden pale look that the chancellor cast upon her stop her?

"No, Annie," she said. "I still have work to do here."

And that was that.

It was strange, Annie reflected on the train the next day, that although she and the chancellor chatted generally of this and that all the way to London, although she found him to be a charming companion, she was surprised that he did not seem to want to talk about women's rights, or indeed, refer to Miss Hammond at all.

She hesistated a little when he offered to escort her to the D'Oyly Carte Opera Company on the following night. It was a special charity production, he said, of "The Pirates of Penzance." All at once she accepted. He was a gentleman – which is more than could be said of her husband!

Chapter Five

IT was two more weeks before the marquess returned to London. And those two weeks had made a great difference to his wife. She had become accustomed to the house and the servants in St. James's Square. She had discovered the pleasures of shopping and sightseeing by herself. And she had several very pleasant outings with the chancellor of the exchequer. He rarely discussed politics with her, and when she had asked him point-blank what he thought about women getting the vote, a subject that was beginning to interest her strongly, he turned the subject aside with, "It is too serious a matter to go into at the moment. I would prefer to talk about something else."

He was comfortable company in that it was somehow like going out with no one. She was not aware of him as a man, only as a quiet, often witty escort whom she forgot about as soon as she had left him.

Marigold, of course, got wind of her friendship with Mr. Shaw-Bufford and promptly called to tell Annie that the whole of London was talking about them. But this Annie knew to be untrue. She had quickly made a few friends among the society women who had viewed her friendship with the chancellor with equanimity, and since all were high sticklers, Annie knew that they would not hesitate to caution her if she were doing anything wrong.

She was quickly becoming accustomed to the life of an independent married woman. No Marigold around day and night to taunt and sneer, no Nanny or Miss Higgins to reprimand, no parents to make her feel rejected by their lack of interest. For it seemed as if her mother and father's sudden burst of affection for her had died the day after she was married. The countess had not even considered it strange that the marquess should leave for France on his own. A woman was not supposed to question her husband's mode of conduct. A good wife was a submissive wife. Any other attitude led to conflict.

It was something of a shock, therefore, when Annie walked into the breakfast room one morning to find her husband calmly eating toast and marmalade and reading the morning papers.

He was wearing a magnificent dressing gown, and his black hair was still tousled from sleep. He grinned at her amiably, remarked that it was a fine morning, and buried his head in his newspaper again.

Annie drank her coffee with angry little sips and glared at what she could see of her husband. "Did you enjoy your stay in Paris?" she asked at last, her voice thin and hard.

He put the paper down. "Very," he remarked. "I didn't spend the whole summer there, of course. I've been down to my country place to look over things for the last month at least."

"You've been . . . and you never thought to write or . . . But you *couldn't* have been there. Marigold sent me a French newspaper cutting with a photograph of you and a Miss S."

"She's late with the news, isn't she?" said the marquess amiably. "That photograph was taken at least a month ago – in fact, it must have been six or seven weeks ago."

Annie put down her coffee cup and placed her hands on the table. "And *who* is Miss S.?" she demanded in a harsh voice.

"Friend of mine," remarked her husband. "And, talking about friends, I hear you've been moving in political circles. Or rather Mr.

Shaw-Bufford's circles. Where on earth did you meet him? I can't see my parents giving him house room."

"I met him at Britlingsea."

"Britlingsea! Good Heavens! What were you doing in a dead-alive dump like that?"

"Perkins recommended it." Perkins was the butler.

"Oh, *that* explains it. You shouldn't listen to Perkins. He's a terrible snob. You must have been bored to death. Anyway, did a confirmed bachelor like Shaw-Bufford simply walk up to you and introduce himself?"

"No, I went to his house."

"Curiouser and curiouser. Who introduced you?"

"A Miss Mary Hammond."

"Never heard of her," pursued the marquess, his irritating good humor unimpaired. "What does she do?"

Anyone the marquess had not heard of must "do" something since anyone he had not heard of could not possibly just "be" someone.

Annie flushed, remembering her man-hating madness.

"She's got something or other to do with Votes for Women," she said awkwardly.

"Indeed? Well, be very careful. I don't want to have to bail you out if you're going to take up smashing shop windows and sniping at trains."

"I should have known you would sneer," said Annie hotly.

"I'm not sneering, my love. I am simply disapproving of some of the militant methods that have been used. For my part, I think women should get the vote. But to return to the question of Mr. Shaw-Bufford, what does he want from you?"

"My company," said Annie coldly.

"He is a most ambitious man and I would have said he did not like women at all, particularly young and pretty ones. Has he asked you for any money?"

"No. How dare you . . . how could . . .?"

"He will," said the marquess equably, picking up his newspaper.

Now Annie had meant to ask her husband why he had married her in a reasonable, grown-up, woman-of-the-world manner. But his careless good nature, his lack of contrition for having abandoned her for so long, made her control snap completely and she fairly screamed at him, "Why did you marry me? Why? Was it solely to humiliate me? *Or was it for my money?*"

He lowered his paper again. For one split second, his eyes looked as cold as ice, but in the next he was his old amiable self again.

'I thought I knew," he said. "But I have not such clear-cut motives as you yourself.

"I? I have not said anything on the subject."

"If my memory serves me right, you told me that you married me simply to get revenge on your sister."

He studied her thoughtfully as her eyelashes fell to veil her expressive eyes.

"I must have been drunk," she whispered.

"Oh, you were," he said sweetly. "You were, indeed. But your voice had the ring of truth. So I decided that, having given you what you wanted, I would make myself scarce."

Annie writhed in misery. Then her anger came back. "You should have *told* me," she snapped. "You should have *said* something. Not simply gone away."

"Did you miss me?" he asked curiously.

Annie lowered her eyes again. "I was too furious to know what I felt."

He gave a cavernous yawn and then picked up the paper. "I do love these marital discussions," he murmured. "They do clear the air. Are we going to the ballet tonight? I seem to recollect that I have tickets somewhere."

Annie blushed. "I – I h-ave promised to go with Mr. Shaw-Bufford," she said miserably.

"Don't worry," he said from behind his newspaper. "I'm sure I can find someone else."

"I'm sure you can," Annie flashed back bitterly.

The door opened. "Lady Marigold Sinclair," announced Perkins.

"We are not at home, Perkins," said the marquess, without even bothering to look up.

"Very good, my lord."

Annie looked at her husband in awe and admiration. "Is it as easy as that?"

He put down his newspaper. "Oh, yes. You don't have to bother about people you don't like, particularly at this time of the day. Anyway, she's probably come to tell you about her engagement."

"*Engagement!*"

"I heard at the club that young Bellamy was about to pop the question."

"But Harry Bellamy is only an Honorable!"

"And since you always compete, you are surprised she settled for less than a duke? Ah, but there's the question of an heir, you see. Since she has already gone out of her way to hire a private detective to find out about my . . . er . . . pleasures, she is probably convinced that she will be got with child first."

"Hired a . . . Oh, even Marigold . . ."

"Surely you did not think that Marigold was in the habit of reading the French newspapers, did you?"

"I'll sue her, I'll murder her, I'll . . ."

"Well, before you do all that, perhaps you might allow me to read my newspaper? I have been reading this same line over and over again."

Annie sat and watched him in smoldering silence. How dare he make her feel so guilty! How dare he sit there calmly after that horrible revelation!

Gradually, she began to plan her day. She would collect her new gown from the dressmaker herself and wear it that very evening. And she would not sit around waiting for her husband to notice her. She would take herself for a drive in the park and show the fashionable world that the Marchioness of Torrance did not care in the slightest that her husband had come home!

The day was gray and mournful. The leaves in the city never seemed to blaze with the red and gold of autumn but simply to crinkle up to a dreary brown.

Still, she felt very *mondaine* as she sat in the marquess's open carriage with the splendid coachman in front and the two enormous footmen at the back.

And then, all at once, she recognized Aunt Agatha's coachman seated on the box of a carriage approaching down Ladies Mile from the other direction.

She called to her coachman to stop and the Winter carriage promptly stopped alongside, so she and Marigold were eyeball to eyeball, so to speak, each dressed to the nines and sitting in their open landaus.

Marigold was seated beside a willowy young man who had a thick, fair moustache. Annie recognized the Honorable Harry Bellamy.

"Congratulate us, sis," cooed Marigold, all feminine flutterings. "Our engagement will be in the newspapers tomorrow."

"I should *kill* you," said Annie, "for having the cheek to set a detective on my husband."

"But how did you . . .?" began Marigold, and then blushed a guilty red.

Annie's temper snapped. She was carrying a frivolous little parasol, closed and held beside her because of the absence of sun. "I *hate* you!" hissed Annie, getting to her feet and standing up in the perilously swaying landau.

Carriages halted beside them, lorgnettes were raised, rouged lips whispered behind fans. "Yes, I hate you," repeated Annie, deaf and blind to the watching crowd.

Marigold shrank back artistically against

Harry Bellamy. "You always were jealous of me," she said.

"Oh, I say. I *say*," bleated Harry Bellamy.

"And what's more," said Marigold, rising to her feet, her eyes glittering, "everyone knows you married Torrance out of spite."

Annie looked ready to leap into her sister's carriage and strangle her. Her coachman flashed a look of mute appeal to the coachman in Marigold's carriage, and both drivers promptly set their teams in motion. Both sisters crashed back down into their seats and, turning their heads, glared at each other.

At last Annie jerked her head around. She became aware of the curious stares from the carriages on either side.

What a scene! Her husband would hear of it. He would hear how his marchioness had behaved like a scullery maid, standing up in her carriage, shouting at her sister, broadcasting to the world at large that Marigold had hired a detective to follow him.

She felt very small and silly.

The Marquess of Torrance held back the curtain of the study window and looked thoughtfully at his wife descending from the carriage. Color was flaming in her cheeks and she looked like an angry kitten. His coachman looked flurried and harassed.

He wondered what on earth she had been up to.

Annie did not see her husband. She did not even know he was in the house. All she wanted to do was to escape to the privacy of her room. The coachman would tell the other servants, the servants would be shocked, and one of the upper servants might consider it all in the line of duty to tell the master.

Why had she not just congratulated Harry Bellamy and Marigold in a dignified way? She searched around for something to distract her. Then she decided to try on her new purchase, which was a wickedly seductive French corset. She realized she had given Barton the day off, but it would be better to try it on by herself without Barton or one of the housemaids wondering if her ladyship had gone mad. For the corset was black, and everyone knew that ladies *never* wear black underwear. But Annie had fallen in love with it. She had dropped in at Maison Lucy in Bond Street after she had collected her gown. They were having a fashion show of all the latest underwear. Annie could never quite get used to seeing all those haughty mannequins wearing underwear *over* plain black dresses – since for decency's sake, they could hardly model it any other way – and

106

often wondered if they felt as ludicrous as they looked.

But her eye had been caught by the corset. It was, first of all, a sensation because it *was* black. A naughty, frivolous thing ornamented with *eau de nil* roses on the garters and fine black lace at the bosom. It was shorter than the long Empire corset that Annie usually wore since it only came down to the top of the thighs. Feeling very daring and wicked, she had bought one.

After she had bathed and brushed out her hair, Anie slipped on the corset and managed to lace herself into it without much trouble.

Then she fastened a pair of cobweb-fine black silk stockings on to the garters. She did not dream of going to the looking glass to study the effect because she had not yet put on her drawers and to see herself in such a stage of undress would be far from ladylike.

She was about to cross the room to the chest of drawers to look for the rest of her under-wear when a familiar, lazy, amused voice from the doorway said, "Very fetching."

The marquess, wearing, as far as her shocked eyes could see, nothing more than his dressing gown, was studying her with appreciative interest.

Annie let out a scream and rushed wildly

about looking for her wrapper, miserably conscious that she was wearing only the corset, her stockings, and a pair of high-heeled evening shoes.

He took two quick steps across the room and caught her in his arms.

"What are you doing?" Annie flamed.

"Competing with Marigold."

"You're mad."

"Not in the slightest. I am in a baby-making mood. I said to myself, I said, why should Marigold's offspring get all that lovely money?"

"Let me go—"

His mouth had covered hers and he was forcing her back towards the bed. She fought and struggled and scratched, but he clipped her hands behind her back and knocked her back across the bed with the simple tactic of falling on top of her.

"Now," he said, "I am going to carry on exactly from where I left off on our wedding night."

The fight went out of Annie as her treacherous body burned and throbbed under an onslaught of kisses and caresses. Probing, clever, sensitive hands moved here and there, causing her sudden, sharp pain and making her cry out, and then somehow causing her to wind her arms tightly about him.

At one point he put a hand behind him, took off her shoes, and threw them across the room. "Your heels are making holes in my back," he complained before moving again, inside her, over her, always holding back until she called his name in the high, sharp tone of complete abandon.

"Now," said the Marquess of Torrance, thoughtfully, "I shall remove this very fetching corset, and since I began at the end, so to speak, I will go back to the beginning."

"You are snoring. Wake up!"

Annie awoke with a jerk. She almost expected to find herself in her husband's arms, but she was in Mr. Shaw-Bufford's box at the ballet and she could see his pale eyes glaring at her in the dim light.

"I'm sorry," she whispered, trying to focus her eyes on the stage. "I'm tired."

Annie had never felt more exhausted in her life. Her husband had finally given her a light kiss on the nose and had left her to struggle into yet another bath. The wreck of the pretty black corset lay in ruins in the corner where it had been thrown.

It had been like a slap in the face to go downstairs eventually, dressed and ready, to find that her husband had already left.

And he had not said one word of love to her.

She could tell at a glance when Mr. Shaw-Bufford arrived to collect her that he was not pleased with her appearance.

She had put on very heavy white makeup, not only on her face but on her chest and arms. There was an enormous love bite on her neck that she had tried to disguise.

And now she had disgraced her escort by falling asleep and snoring.

The lights on the stage and the darkness of the theater made her yawn and yawn, and she was relieved when the interval came.

Relieved until she saw her husband in a box opposite with a very handsome, dark-haired woman. Not once did the marquess look around the theater to see if Annie was there. Annie felt a lump rising in her throat, and Mr. Shaw-Bufford looked at her with increasing irritation.

He had heard of the fight in the park – who had not? He was an ambitious man and he did not want to have his name coupled with that of a woman who behaved so disgracefully. But he needed Lady Torrance for just one thing . . .

Annie did not look at the stage once for the rest of the performance. She studied her husband and his companion through her opera glasses, searching for some sign of intimacy. There was no doubt that his companion was a lady and that made her doubly dangerous in Annie's eyes.

Mr. Shaw-Bufford was anxious to be alone with Annie to ask one all-important question. He had told the driver to take them back to St. James's Square the long way around.

Annie was too tired to notice that they were heading down Northumberland Avenue instead of going through Trafalgar Square and along Pall Mall. She did not notice anything until they were passing the Houses of Parliament. The square in front seemed to be full of women, silent women, hundreds and hundreds of them, just sitting or standing.

"What on earth are they doing?" she asked.

"They're keeping a silent vigil," said Mr. Shaw-Bufford indifferently. "They're the non-militant women who want the vote."

Annie looked out at them in wonder as the carriage passed through Parliament Square. She found the spectacle very moving; all those women, standing out in the cold, so quietly, so silently.

"Lady Torrance," began Mr. Shaw-Bufford, edging closer to her on the carriage seat. "There's something I wish . . ."

"Poor things," said Annie, still looking out

and not hearing him. "Poor things. And yet how I admire them."

Mr. Shaw-Bufford rapped on the roof of the brougham with his cane. "Why are we going in the wrong direction, man?" he called to the driver. "St. James's Square immediately."

Then he leaned back, a smile beginning to curve his thin lips. For all at once he knew how to get Annie to give him what he wanted.

Annie said good night to her companion and climbed the stairs, desperate for sleep. But although she slept deeply and heavily, she awoke suddenly in the middle of the night and began to burn with jealousy – although she did not recognize the emotion for what it was.

She imagined her husband lying in bed with the dark-haired woman in his arms, doing all those delicious things to her that he had done to Annie.

The nightmare seemed to become reality, and all at once she was sure he had taken the dark-haired woman to his room. He was holding her, and they were both laughing about the stupidity of the silly little marchioness.

She lit the bed candle and, seizing it, walked out into the corridor. The door to her husband's suite was at the other side of the stairs. She walked silently along and gently turned the handle of the door. It would not budge. Locked! And there could only be one reason for her husband locking the door.

Rage burned in her. Fury. Hate. If he thought he was going to lie in there enjoying his extramarital lust, then he had another think coming!

She walked into an adjoining bathroom, picked up a hand towel, and carefully stuffed it along the bottom of his door. Then she bent down and lit it with the candle. It burned badly but created a lot of nasty smoke, which was just what Annie wanted.

She retreated to the top of the stairs and started to scream at the top of her lungs, "Fire! Fire! Help! Help!"

There was the thud of feet as the first of the servants pounded down from the attic. Soon the whole house was alive with running, terrified people.

Perkins ran down the street in his nightshirt, howling for the fire brigade, before he remembered he could have used the telephone.

Annie had put on her dressing gown. She had wanted to keep watch on the marquess's door to see the guilty pair emerge, but Perkins, already seeing the morning headlines, "Butler Saves Noble Family," had forced her to go out into the street while he ran back to rouse the master.

But the fire brigade arrived on the scene, horses steaming, bell clanging, and would not allow Perkins his moment of glory. Without waiting to see if there was any smoke or flames, they began to run the hose into the house. The towel under the marquess's door smoldered on and only a small trickle of smoke was escaping. It was enough for the fire chief. "Here, men!" he called. They ran the hose up the stairs. At last the marquess, aroused by the commotion, opened his bedroom door (it was inclined to stick and had not been locked at all) and received a cascade of water full in the chest.

Well, it seemed as if everyone was trying to shout explanations to his lordship. But his lordship did not seem to be listening to anyone because he had picked up a piece of charred towel from the doorway and was looking at it thoughtfully. Then he saw the bed candle on its flat stand lying on the floor a little distance away.

"Whose candle is that, Bessie?" he asked one of the housemaids.

"It's her ladyship's," said Bessie. "See, it's got a rose design, my lord, to match my lady's room."

"It seems as if we have brought you out all because of a false alarm," said the marquess, with unimpaired amiability, to the fire chief. "Bessie, fetch Perkins and see that the gentlemen of the fire department are given a tankard of beer apiece and something for their trouble. Where is her ladyship?"

"My lady is out on the street with the servants, my lord," said Bessie. "I would be out there with them if I had got up in time, but I'm such a heavy sleeper."

"Fetch her ladyship and bring us something warm to drink in the study. Tell the servants to clean this room and light a fire to dry the place out."

The marquess retreated into his rooms, changed into a black polo jumper and an old pair of flannel bags, and made his way to the study.

Annie was warming her toes at a newly lit fire. She was leaning forward so that the curtain of her red hair hid her face from him.

He sat down opposite, and she gave him a scared, guilty look and dropped her eyes again.

"Don't say a word until I have had a good stiff drink," he said. "Ah, Perkins! There you are. Well, as you see, there was no fire, but it shows that you can do splendidly in an emergency. How much would you like me to give you?"

"Since there was no fire, my lord, I would say that ten pounds would be very generous."

"So would I, Perkins. So would I. But I can only assume that there is something you wish to buy that you have your heart set on. You will find the money in the desk over there. Help yourself. And then bring me something to make some punch."

"Thank you, my lord. Very good, my lord."

When the butler had left, Annie said, "Do you *always* ask your servants how much money they want as a tip?"

"Oh, always," he said. "They never ask for too much. People like to be trusted."

"I like to trust people," said Annie, in a low voice.

Perkins arrived with a tray bearing a bottle of whiskey, lemons, brown sugar, a jug of hot water, and a punch bowl, which he set on a small table and then placed it in front of his master. Then he bowed and withdrew.

Annie watched her husband nervously as he mixed the punch. Then she found she could keep silent no longer.

"Well, it was only a false alarm," she said brightly. "I wonder what caused that smoke? I'm afraid I panicked. I was sure you would be burned to death."

"Really?" he said, seeming to concentrate his whole attention on the punch. "Annie, why did you set a towel alight and push it under my door?"

"I didn't," lied Annie, feeling a telltale blush creeping up her neck and face.

"You did, you know. I'm sorry if my love-making upset you so much that you felt compelled to set fire to me."

Annie looked at him miserably. He gave her a charming smile and handed her a steaming glass.

"Do I have to tell you?" asked Annie.

"No," he said gently. "I am sure you have some perfectly reasonable explanation. Perhaps it's a well-known Scotch custom, like setting the heather on fire."

"Oh, I'll tell you," said Annie, cradling her glass in her hands. "I tried your door and I thought it was locked, and therefore I thought you had the infernal cheek to bring that dark-haired woman home to bed with you."

"What? Polly? My first cousin? Never. Come to think of it, I've never brought any of my lady friends here."

"Your cousin?"

"Yes. Mrs. Jimmy Waite-Hansen – Polly. You met her at our wedding reception."

"I didn't remember . . ."

"Anyway, why the fire?"

"I was trying to smoke you out."

He laughed and laughed. Finally he mopped his streaming eyes. "Jealousy is a wonderful thing," he said.

"I? Jealous?" said Annie, feeling hurt and humiliated. "You have to be in love with someone to be jealous. I was merely incensed at the thought that you had brought one of your many mistresses back here."

"Of course," he agreed amiably. "I had forgotten. Yes, do you know that for one little space of time, I had forgotten that you did not marry me for love."

She looked at him, searching for the courage to tell him that she had not meant that remark about marrying him merely to get revenge on Marigold. But it had been true. *Was* true. Or was it? Oh, she didn't know *what* she felt, she thought wretchedly, and somehow the moment to say anything had passed and he was saying mildly, "You look exhausted. You had better go to bed."

Again she hesitated, wanting to say something. But he had never said that he loved her. And probably Marigold was right and he had married her for her money. Hadn't he only made love to her just to beget a child before

Marigold?

With a mumbled "Good night," she trailed from the room, hesitating at each step, hoping that he would call her back.

But he sat very still beside the fire, his glass in his hand, looking into the flames.

She did not see him at all the next day. By evening, a servant handed her a ribboned box and a long envelope. The box contained a bottle of perfume called Night in Paris. The envelope contained a letter from her husband, saying that he had been called down to the country to settle a boundary dispute and would be back within a few days.

She stared mutinously at the perfume. She would not open it, would not wear it. He was her husband. He should have taken her with him. He did not love her. She had turned down two social engagements for the evening because – because she had a headache, she told herself fiercely. She would not even admit it to herself, her pride would not allow it, that she had stayed home simply to see him again.

Like the heavy feet of the prisoners on the treadmill at Newgate, her thoughts churned laboriously around and around in her head until she decided sadly that he had not gone to the country, that he was probably lying in the experienced arms of some mistress, and that he was not thinking of her at all.

For the next three days she threw herself into a frenzy of social activities that left her feeling tired and listless.

On the morning of the fourth day, Miss Mary Hammond called. At first Annie debated whether to see her or not. Then she remembered that Mr. Shaw-Bufford had not seemed to disapprove of Miss Hammond, so perhaps she was not quite as mad as she had appeared at the meeting in the Masonic Hall.

Miss Hammond's appearance was reassuring. She was wearing a smart felt hat and a walking dress, which, although not precisely fashionable, at least looked like a woman's dress.

"My dear Annie," began Miss Hammond, as Annie walked into the drawing room. "What a charming home you have! That's what I came to talk to you about."

"Pray sit down," said Annie, ringing the bell and asking for the tea tray. "Surely you did not come simply to tell me how charming my home is!"

"No." Miss Hammond gave an awkward laugh. "I'll get straight to the point. I don't believe in shilly-shallying. I have formed a little band of women supporters. Your town house is so central. I wondered if you would consider helping our cause by holding a meeting here?"

"Here!" Annie looked about her. She wanted to say that she would feel easier in her mind if she asked her husband's permission, but that would probably be taken by Miss Hammond to betray a weak-kneed slavish dependency.

"Are you still sort of . . . well, 'Down with Men' and all that?" she asked.

"Well, no," said Miss Hammond, baring her large teeth in a smile. "Men are in power at the moment and we need their support. But Our Day Will Come."

"So what is the purpose . . .?"

"The Vote."

"Oh," said Annie doubtfully. "You do not plan anything *militant* . . .?"

"Oh, no, no. We have Other Means."

For a moment, Miss Hammond's pale eyes flashed, and Annie felt increasingly nervous.

"Do I know any of the ladies perhaps?" she asked, to stall for time.

"I think at least one name will be familiar to you. Mrs. Amy Cartwright."

Annie's face cleared. "I know Mrs. Cartwright well," she said. Amy Cartwright was a young widow and one of Annie's newfound social friends.

"And Mrs. Tommy Winton."

Better still. Mrs. Winton was a frivolous matron.

"Very well," said Annie, slowly. "And when is this meeting to take place?"

"I thought perhaps Saturday."

"*This* Saturday?"

"I know it's short notice." Miss Hammond played her ace. "Mr. Shaw-Bufford was sure you would not mind and he has promised to look in."

"Well, I have no arrangements for Saturday afternoon, but perhaps Saturday evening was what you had in mind?"

"Oh, no. Saturday afternoon at two o'clock. We are having a meeting to arrange a social function to raise funds."

Annie smiled with relief. She had been afraid that the purpose of the meeting was to arrange some sort of *painful* demonstration like chaining themselves to the railings of the Houses of Parliament.

"What a pleasant way of raising money." She smiled. Secretly, Annie found herself hoping that her husband would return in time for the meeting. Then he would see that she had ideals, that she was not a useless member of society, unfit to set foot on his precious estates. For, among her other fears, Annie was beginning to wonder whether her husband was ashamed of her.

She imagined him entering the drawing room and finding her presiding over a meeting of intelligent, dedicated women. This happy dream carried her through until Saturday.

Saturday was a gloomy day. Rain fell steadily and remorselessly from a leaden sky. Raindrops trickled down the windows, blurring the view of the buildings across the square.

Annie's throat was sore and her forehead felt hot.

She had not been ill since childhood, and she refused to accept the fact that she was ill now. She moved hazily through the house supervising the arrangements for the meeting: arranging flowers in bowls, telling the servants to carry in ranks of chairs from the drawing room, cajoling the cook into preparing her special scones for the occasion.

At times she couldn't stop shivering and asked for fires to be lit throughout the house; then she was boiling hot and fretfully told the servants to open all the windows.

By the time the ladies started to arrive,

shaking dripping umbrellas in the hall, Annie found that her vision was becoming slightly blurred and the day had begun to take on a dreamlike quality. She was too busy supervising the serving of tea to take in much of what was going on. Although she was the hostess, the women seemed to have forgotten about her.

Mrs. Tommy Winton was enthusiastically discussing arrangements for a ball to be held in her house. With the exception of Miss Hammond and a few of her militant supporters, the other ladies were mostly society butterflies who were supporting the Vote for Women movement as the latest fad and who were more interested in an excuse to hold a ball than in any political reform.

After a date had been fixed and caterers agreed on, Miss Hammond rose to make her speech. With amazing fervor, she thanked the ladies who had gathered to support her. By the evening of the ball, she said, she hoped to be able to tell them Marvelous News at which they would Throw Off Their Chains. Her audience, in the main, listened with polite disinterest. Miss Hammond and her society were merely part of the excuse for the ball and something to be endured on a rainy afternoon.

The butler murmured in Annie's ear as she

was just sitting down that Mr. Shaw-Bufford had arrived and begged a few words with her in private.

Annie arose wearily. Her head was on fire and her legs felt as heavy as lead. She followed Perkins to the study where Mr. Shaw-Bufford had taken up a position before the fire.

After a few preliminary conversational gambits, he got down to brass tacks.

"Lady Torrance," he said, taking her hand in his, his deep-set eyes boring down into Annie's fevered ones. "I am deeply moved to find that you have given up your house to such a noble cause. I have never discussed politics with you. But I will tell you this in the deepest confidence because I feel there is a bond of friendship between us . . ."

He hesitated, waiting for some response. He noticed Annie's scarlet face and, not realizing it was the result of fever, put it down as a gratified blush.

"If I were prime minister," he said in a low voice, "then women would have the vote, I assure you."

Annie tried to gather her scrambled wits. "But Mr. Macleod is prime minister," she said, passing the hand he was not holding over her hot brow.

"Exactly. And while he is in power there is

not much I can do. That position should have been mine. But the day will come . . . Forgive me, I go too fast. The fact is, this society of Miss Hammond's needs money. With money we can start to gain power."

"But . . . the ball," said Annie, weakly. "That is to raise money."

"All it will raise is interest in the movement," he said dryly. "By the time all the arrangements are paid for out of the subscriptions, there will be little left.

"And that is what has given me the courage to approach you. Lady Torrance, I beg you to contribute ten thousand pounds to the society."

"What?" said Annie, dizzily. She tugged her hand away. "My dear Mr. Shaw-Bufford, you must ask my husband."

"But you are a wealthy heiress. Surely you have money of your own?"

"I don't know," said Annie, wretchedly. "All my husband told me was that he had made arrangements for me to draw money on his bank any time I wanted."

"Then it is probably your money. Your husband's life-style, dear Lady Torrance, is . . . But I must not say more. It is *your* money, believe me. You are not his slave. You are an independent lady."

By this time Annie would have paid him double the amount to get rid of him, she felt so ill. "I – I must think," she said. "When shall I give you the money?"

"Well, I do not wish to rush you. Shall we say next Wednesday? I shall call for tea."

"Yes, yes," said Annie. "Now I really must get back to my guests . . ."

"Of course," he said smoothly. He walked forward and held the door of the study open for her. "Perhaps you would be so good as to send Miss Hammond to me, Lady Torrance? That is, if she has finished speaking."

Annie nodded and went out. She entered the drawing room and gave Miss Hammond the chancellor's message.

It was only when Miss Hammond had left and Annie looked around the room through glazed and feverish eyes that she began to feel resentful. Mrs. Tommy Winton had taken over the role of hostess and was ordering the servants about as if she were in her own house. Nobody bothered to pay Annie the least attention.

To add to that, thought Annie furiously, the chancellor was holding private meetings in her husband's study and sending the lady of the house scurrying about on his errands like a servant girl.

Well, he would stop it this instant!

Annie marched in the direction of the study. But as she put her hand on the doorknob, the intensity of the two voices inside the room stopped her. She was also assailed by a feeling of giddiness and a pounding in her ears, so the voices from inside the room seemed as if they were rising and falling on the waves of the sea.

"If I am caught, I shall at least be a martyr . . ." boomed Miss Hammond.

Mr. Shaw-Bufford's answer came out in a sort of hiss that nonetheless carried through the panels of the study door.

"You will not be caught, Miss Hammond. Remember, my name must never be mentioned. Never!"

And then the voices sank to a murmur.

Annie turned wearily away. All at once she was too ill to cope. Let them stay till the coming of the Cocqeigrues for all she cared!

Chapter Six

"AND where is my wife, may I ask?" said a pleasant, masculine voice from the doorway of the drawing room.

Mrs. Winton had a mouthful of scone and strawberry jam and could only stare wildly at the Marquess of Torrance in dumb silence. Miss Hammond sailed forward like a tweedy galleon.

"Annie must be somewhere around," she said brightly.

"Annie? You mean my wife, Lady Torrance?"

"Yes. You must not think me presumptuous, my lord, but dear Annie simply begged me to call her by her Christian name."

The marquess leaned one broad shoulder against the doorway and smiled benignly at the room full of women.

For some reason they all found themselves becoming ruffled and uncomfortable.

Mrs. Winton succeeded in gulping down her scone. "Lady Torrance was here a moment ago," she said, peering around hopefully. Everyone began to look around in a ludicrous way as if the Marchioness of Torrance were a missing handbag.

"Then," pursued the marquess, "since you cannot produce my wife, perhaps you can enlighten me as to why so many of you delightful ladies have called for tea."

"It's a meeting. We're organizing a ball to raise funds to support the Vote for Women movement," volunteered Mrs. Winton, after a short silence in which no one spoke.

"And it was my wife's idea?"

"Well, no," blustered Miss Hammond. "I asked dear Ann – Lady Torrance if we could use her house and she said we could. Of course, she is a devoted supporter."

"Obviously a strong feminist," said the marquess sweetly, "since my house has become not 'our' house but *her* house."

"Oh, your lordship will have your little joke."

"Yes, I will, won't I. Ah, Shaw-Bufford! Have you just arrived?"

The chancellor had been trying to glide silently through the hall behind the marquess's back, but somehow the marquess, in some peculiar way, had seemed to sense he was there without turning his head.

He came to stand beside the marquess in the open doorway.

"Perhaps you can tell me the whereabouts of my wife?" asked the marquess.

"I was talking to her a little moment ago. I sent her to fetch Miss Hammond and bring her to see me in the study. I . . ." His voice trailed off under the marquess's look of bland surprise.

"Then perhaps you sent her scurrying off on

another little errand? Dear me. Is it the servants' day off by any chance? No, it can't be. I quite distinctly see several of them at least, ministering to all your needs."

"My lord, I—"

"So I suppose I had better look for her myself." The marquess ambled off after bestowing another sweet smile on all and sundry.

There was an awkward silence. Mr. Shaw-Bufford collected his hat, cane, and long gray coat with the astrakhan collar. Two little spots of color burned on his cheeks. He could never understand why such a useless dilettante as the Marquess of Torrance always contrived to make him feel ridiculous.

Annie, tossing and turning on her bed in the throes of a fever, felt a cool hand laid on her brow. It was taken away to be replaced by a cloth soaked in iced water and cologne.

"Oh, that's very good, Barton," she mumbled, only to be answered by a masculine voice saying gently, "The doctor will be here soon. Try to lie still."

"Jasper!" she said, reaching out and clutching his sleeve.. "Where are you?"

"I'm here."

"Don't go away!"

"I won't. Be still."

Annie fell into a feverish dream in which Mr. Shaw-Bufford was chasing Miss Hammond through the maze at Hampton Court. "I shan't be caught," Miss Hammond was crying. 'I shall be a martyr instead."

Then she awoke to the murmur of masculine voices, a Scottish one – the doctor? – saying, "Her ladyship has the influenza, my lord. I will go myself to the chemist's and have her medicine made up and return with it directly."

And then Annie plunged back into tortured dreams.

For the next forty-eight hours, it was hard for Annie to separate her dreams from reality. At one time it seemed as if Marigold was in the room, looking down at her with bright, malicious eyes. Marigold was saying shrilly, "Are you sure she is *really* ill? She would always do anything to get attention."

And her husband's voice replying, "Please leave my house and don't dare come back until you are invited."

And sometime later a pleasant sensation of strong hands lifting her into a warm, scented bath, rubbing her down with a fleecy towel, carrying her back to bed again.

And then it seemed, at last, as if she awoke properly. Her head was clear and everything in the room looked sharp and new.

Her husband was sleeping in a chair beside the embers of the fire. He was unshaven and wrapped in his dressing gown.

She lay quietly studying his face. It was much stronger than it usually seemed, devoid as it was in sleep of its indolent charm. The mouth was set in a firm line. Two grooves of weariness were etched from his nostrils down each side of his mouth. His hair was tousled, one thick lock falling over his forehead.

Annie tried to think that his vigil by her bedside was a sign of love but could not bring herself to believe it. She was sure he would also sit up all night in the stables if his favorite horse were sick. And on that cynical thought she fell asleep again, awaking again when the sun was high in the sky.

There was no sign of her husband. The fire was blazing cheerfully, the hearth had been swept, and the curtains pulled back. Great white castles of clouds were being tugged across a chill, blue sky. Of her husband, there was no sign. Annie began to wonder if she had imagined the whole thing.

Barton came in quickly and exclaimed on seeing her mistress awake. "We were very worried about you, my lady," said the maid, coming forward to straighten the pillows behind Annie's head. "Thank the Lord the fever has gone. There's a epidemic of that nasty influenza all over London. People are dropping like flies. I told the master he should hire a nurse, but he insisted on doing all the work himself."

"He did? I didn't dream it?"

"No, my lady. He only went off to get some sleep when he found your fever had gone down. Everyone in London seems to have called, but he wouldn't let anyone see you. Lady Marigold came straight up one day when he was out of the room for a moment, and he was so angry when he found her here."

"I seem to remember something about it," said Annie.

"Mr. Shaw-Bufford called as well," said Barton. "He said to remind your ladyship that you had an engagement on Wednesday. I didn't tell his lordship, for I was sure he would be annoyed. It was thoughtless of Mr. Shaw-Bufford when you are so ill."

Annie flushed guiltily, suddenly remembering with awful clarity her promise to give the chancellor money.

The door opened and her husband strolled in. She searched his face for some sign of love, but his eyes held a strangely guarded look. He sat down on the edge of the bed and studied her face.

"I'm glad to see you well, my dear," he said. "The doctor says you are to continue taking your medicine for the rest of the week and you are to rest in bed. He will be along to see you this afternoon. You gave us quite a fright. When I arrived home I found the house full of chattering women and the chancellor of the exchequer making free with my study.

"It puzzles me that Shaw-Bufford should champion women's rights. I would have said that the only thing that man believed in intensely was the advancement of Shaw-Bufford."

Annie avoided his gaze and plucked nervously at the satin quilt. Barton left the room.

"Now what is worrying you?" teased the marquess. "You have two little lines right in the middle of your forehead."

"I was wondering if I had any money of my own," said Annie, still not meeting his eyes.

There was a little silence. Then the marquess said lightly, "Did I not tell you? Your father deposited a great deal in a private account for you. He wrote to me only the other day about it, but you were too ill to receive the news. Certainly, it's yours . . . as my money is yours."

It was on the tip of Annie's tongue to say that she believed he hadn't any. Instead she said, "Do you have access to my money?"

"No," he said, looking at her steadily, "which is a pity since I have already dissipated your dowry in riotous living. I assume that is what you expect to hear?"

"Yes . . . I mean, no . . . I mean . . . Oh, what would you do if someone asked you for a large sum of money for a certain organization?"

"If I believed in what the organization was doing and I thought they genuinely needed the money, and if I could afford it, then I would certainly give them a check. Them. Not he or she, if you take my meaning. I would take the precaution of making the check out in the name of the organization and not to the individual who asked for it."

"But if it was someone in a high position, someone in a national position of trust . . .? What if, say, King Edward asked you for money for a certain charity?"

"Then I would most definitely insist that the check be made out to the charity," replied the marquess, his eyes crinkling up with laughter.

"Oh." Annie digested this in silence. Then she remembered that Barton had said that Marigold had called. And she also remembered Marigold looking down at her, but it still all seemed part of a fevered dream. And had he meant all that about having spent her dowry on riotous living?

"Barton says Marigold called," she said. "When is she getting married?"

"I neither know nor care."

Annie smiled. "So you were only teasing me . . .?"

"About what, my love?"

Annie blushed. "About wanting me to have a baby before Marigold."

"Well, according to your father, if Marigold has a son, the child will be the heir to the title and fortune since Marigold is the eldest. I felt quite depressed when I heard the news. But, ah well, one can't compete with Marigold forever."

So he didn't love her. How that thought pierced Annie's heart. Her pain made her lash out. "It's just not fair," she said. "No matter what I do, she always seems to win.

He looked at her thoughtfully. Was it her imagination or was there a certain hint of ice in his blue eyes? But the next second he was smiling amiably down at her. He yawned and stretched. "Well, my dear," he said, rising from the bed, "I am glad you are better. I can now toddle off and frivol about London in my usual manner."

"With Miss S.?" said Annie, bitterly.

"Unfortunately, she is still in Paris. Perhaps I shall send her a wire . . ." And with that, he strolled out of the room.

Annie lay, staring out at the cold sky and aching with misery. For the rest of the day, she tortured herself with pictures of her husband walking about London with some pretty charmer or another on his arm. She pictured Marigold's false pity.

In her mind, her husband slowly turned into an evil and depraved monster, and by evening she had conjured up such a Frankenstein that it was something of a shock when the marquess ambled into the room looking very much his usual handsome self.

"What do you want?" said Annie harshly.

"I've come to read to you," he answered mildly, settling himself down in the armchair in front of the fire.

"I don't *want* to be read to," said Annie pettishly. "My head aches."

"Then you will find my voice very soothing," he said imperturbably.

He began to read while Annie lay and seethed with fury. At first she was so angry that she could not hear the words, but after some time, despite herself, she began to listen.

He had chosen Surtees's *Handley Cross*, and Annie's attention was caught by the mad antics of that famous huntsman, Mr. Jorrocks. The marquess read in a rather flat, soothing voice. From time to time Annie would remember her hurt and open her mouth to say something wounding, but somehow she found she could not and began to listen to the story again.

She had just decided that as soon as he finished the next chapter she would tell him what she really thought of him, when all at once it was morning again and she had slept the whole night through.

After that he ambled in and out of her room for the next two days, sometimes chatting to her, sometimes reading to her, always ignoring the blazing hurt and fury in her wide eyes.

Mr. Shaw-Bufford had sent flowers daily; Miss Hammond had sent a large box of chocolates. Marigold contented herself by sending Annie a letter, sympathizing with her sister for having such a tyrannical beast of a husband. Annie sent a letter to Mr. Shaw-Bufford thanking him for the flowers and regretting that she would be unable to see him until she was feeling better.

And then, just as she was feeling fully recovered, just as she was beginning to thaw towards her infuriating husband, just as her slowly maturing brain was beginning to tell her that a man did not spend his days waiting on his wife unless he felt *something* for her, she received a note from him saying that he had gone back to the country.

He begged her to forgive him. He pointed out that the matter was urgent. One of his tenants had been arrested for murder. He had killed another man in a drunken brawl. Although he was undoubtedly guilty, arrangements had to be made for the welfare of his wife and children.

Annie did not believe a word of it.

All at once, it was not Marigold she wished revenge on; it was her husband. She had an intensely feminine longing to play his game and see how *he* liked it.

Her mind shrank from the idea of actually having an affair with anyone. But somehow she was sure she could arrange things so that her husband would *think* that she had fallen in love.

Annie was resting on the sofa in the morning room the day after her husband had left when Mr. Shaw-Bufford was announced.

She toyed with the idea of starting to flirt with the chancellor in order to make her husband jealous and then dismissed it, knowing instinctively that Mr. Shaw-Bufford was the last man to make her husband jealous.

The chancellor came in, wreathed in smiles and flowers. Annie gave his present of a handsome bunch of chrysanthemums to a housemaid to put in a vase and thanked him prettily for all his bouquets and messages.

He told her that the arrangements for the ball were going ahead. It would be held in a week's time at Mrs. Winton's and practically the whole of London society had paid for tickets.

"That's very gratifying," said Annie, surprised. "I did not think so many members of society would be interested in women getting the vote."

"They aren't," said the chancellor. "We simply told them it was in aid of 'Women of the World,' which sounds vague enough to be reassuring."

"Isn't that dishonest?" asked Annie. "I mean, shouldn't you tell them what the ball is really in aid of?"

"Why?" he said baldly. "They wouldn't come if they knew exactly what it was in aid of."

"But Mrs. Winton . . .?"

"Mrs. Winton has already forgotten."

"Does anybody believe in *anything*?" said Annie.

"Of course," he replied, hitching his chair a little closer. "*We* do, Lady Torrance, but we are diplomats. Diplomats! People of our intelligence know that the end justifies the means."

"I don't think I believe that exactly," said Annie.

He patted her hand. "Then you must trust me to believe it for you. May I remind you that you were gracious enough to offer to donate a little something?"

Despite her embarrassment, Annie could not help saying, "Ten thousand pounds is not a 'little something.' "

"Ha! Ha! No, of course not, but, however, you . . ."

"What is the name of Miss Hammond's society?" interrupted Annie, rising and going over to a desk in the corner. "I mean, what is it *really* called now?"

"I believe 'Women's Rights, The Vote, and Feminine Equality.' "

"Dear me. I hope all that will fit on to one line of the checkbook."

"There is no need for that." Mr. Shaw-Bufford smiled. "Simply make out the check to me, and I will see the funds are given to the society."

"No, I couldn't do that," said Annie, stubbornly. "My husband told me never to

142

give money to an individual, always to a society."

"Lady Torrance! That sounds just as if you didn't trust me!"

Annie bit her lip. She could not forget how her husband had asked her whether Shaw-Bufford had approached her for money, and when she had told him that the chancellor had not, the marquess had calmly replied, "He will."

"Why can't I just make the check out to the society?" she asked.

"Because they do not have a banking account in their name yet."

"Then what are they going to do with the money from the ball if they can't bank it?"

"The money will be handed to me. I will put it into a separate account so that Miss Hammond and her supporters may draw on it whenever they wish."

Annie looked very young and feminine in a long tea gown of blond lace. She picked up the checkbook, and Mr. Shaw-Bufford smiled his encouragement.

"I think I should explain something," said Annie, with the open candor of a child. Only her husband would have recognized that look as being a preliminary to a whopping lie.

"I haven't any money of my own. So this

would be my husband's money and he's bound to ask questions."

"You surely did not tell your husband . . .?"

"Oh, no," said Annie gently. "I only discussed the matter with him in general terms. He told me I must never give a check to an individual who was asking for money for some society but only to the society itself. So perhaps if you would like to ask him . . .?"

"But you are a wealthy heiress!" exclaimed the chancellor.

"I'm afraid not." Annie sighed. "Poor papa. He thought he had been left a fortune, but the legacy turned out to be only a few hundred pounds, which, of course, he is keeping for himself. But my husband . . ."

"I have been shamefully misled," said the chancellor stiffly.

"Indeed, Mr. Shaw-Bufford," said Annie coldly. "I thought we were friends."

"But you led me to believe you were an heiress."

"*I* was led to believe I was an heiress," said Annie sweetly. "Now I find I am completely dependent on my husband for every penny. I am doing my best to help you, Mr. Shaw-Bufford. If there is nothing, er, about your request for money that is strange, then I do not

144

see why you do not ask my husband. You will find him extremely sympathetic towards the feminist movement."

"In that case, let us forget about the whole thing," said Mr. Shaw-Bufford sourly.

"Will you stay for tea?" Annie stretched a hand out toward the bell.

"No," he said harshly. "I have another appointment."

"Then I shall see you at the ball," replied Annie.

Mr. Shaw-Bufford hesitated in the doorway. "Since I have no intention of approaching your husband for the money, Lady Torrance, I beg you to keep the matter a secret between us."

"Of course," said Annie, opening her eyes very wide.

"Then good day to you, my lady."

After he had gone, Annie sat down, feeling a bit weak in the knees. Marigold, she felt, would never have got herself into such a ridiculous situation as turning down the chancellor of the exchequer. Then it began to strike her as amusing that the chancellor of the exchequer should try to borrow money from *her*. And then, after her amusement, she began to wonder seriously why the chancellor of the exchequer should be in need of money.

After turning this problem over and over in

her mind and finding no solution, she began to think of ways to show her husband that she did not care for him.

And then she had a splendid idea. She would flirt with Harry Bellamy, Marigold's fiancé, and that way she would be revenged on two birds, Marigold and her husband.

Annie was still very young. She had not realized that she was deeply in love with her husband. She had not realized that Marigold was not worth the trouble.

Annie felt small and humiliated and alone in a hostile world. Her cold, aloof mother was of no help. Miss Winter appeared to have forgotten about her niece as soon as the marriage ceremony was over. Perhaps if she had had intimate friends to talk to, it might have made her life easier. But the society women she took tea with and chatted to at balls and parties were the kind that Annie knew instinctively would betray a confidence at the first possible opportunity. She never stopped to consider that her choice of friends was unfortunate. Her experience with women – her mother, her nanny, her governess, her sister, and her aunt – had made her think that the whole human race consisted of hanging judges.

So she bitterly turned her plan of revenge

over in her head and saw nothing wrong with it.

To Annie it seemed as if everything was going her way.

Her husband had returned from the country in time to escort her to the ball, and Marigold and Harry Bellamy were to be present at it.

The marquess did not return until the morning of the day of the ball and seemed almost surprised by the enthusiastic reception he received from his wife. Annie had been frightened that he would be delayed and that her marvelous plan would have to be left until another time.

The day was foggy. It started with a thin fog in the morning, with a little red disk of a sun moving above it. Then in the afternoon it turned from gray to a thick, blackish yellow, and by evening it was a regular "pea souper." It was freezing fog, too, riming the railings and pavements with hoarfrost.

The fog added to Annie's feelings of excitement and anticipation: the bitter, smoky, autumn smell of it; the feeling of secrecy in the veiled streets outside.

Carriage lights flickered like fireflies through the gloom of the square outside as the fog swayed and thinned a little before thickening again and pressing against the windowpanes.

Fog had crept into the house in St. James's Square and lay in thick strata across the hall as Annie descended the staircase with Barton behind her carrying her evening cloak.

She was wearing a mauve silk evening skirt that rustled as she walked. Her blouse was of paler mauve lace, cut low over the bosom, and with pagoda sleeves. Around her neck she wore a thin band of black velvet holding her locket. Her fine, silky red hair had been dressed in a new style, gently waved over her brow and dressed in a chignon at the back and threaded with white silk flowers that were shaded at the edges with violet.

The door of the drawing room opened and her husband came out to meet her. Annie felt a queer little pain at her heart. She had forgotten how superb he looked in evening dress, with the gleaming white of his shirt setting off his handsome, tanned face.

His eyes had a strangely hooded look as he watched her descend. Annie waited for him to compliment her on her appearance, but he remained silent, merely taking her heavy black evening cloak trimmed with ermine and putting it about her shoulders. Did his hands remain on her shoulders for longer than was necessary?

But the next minute he was being helped into his own coat by Perkins and putting his silk hat on his head. The diamond studs on his shirtfront sparkled and flashed fire like the forst on the pavement outside.

He helped her into the brougham, then raised the trap in the roof with his cane and called to the coachman, "Do you think you can find your way? It's a filthy night!"

"Think I'll manage all right, m'lord," came the coachman's voice. "I'll take her nice and slow."

The marquess settled back against the leather upholstery as the coach began to edge its way through the fog-shrouded streets.

He pulled his coat tightly across his shirt. "Otherwise it will be filthy before we get there," he said as if answering a question. And then, in the same tone of voice, he went on, "It's a mercy that our prime minister is still alive! Certainly if Mrs. Winton had not changed the name of the society to Women of the World, I am sure that, in the circumstances, the ball would have to be canceled. As it is . . ."

"What happened? I don't know what on earth you're talking about?"

"Jimmy Macleod, our prime minister, was

nearly killed today." The marquess's voice came out of the darkness of the carriage. "Some woman shot at him as he left the House. His papers had slipped from the seat of his carriage, so he bent down to pick them up. As he did so, a bullet whizzed over his head and buried itself in the upholstery.

"Whoever fired at him was an expert marksman – or markswoman rather. If he had not bent over at that precise moment, he would most certainly have been killed."

"Did they catch the woman?"

"No," said the marquess. "She escaped into the thick fog. A man saw her briefly. All he could say was that she was heavy-set and heavily veiled. She was carrying a rifle, which she thrust under her coat. You may not find your friend Miss Hammond at the ball tonight. The police are rounding up all the militant feminists in London."

"Well, it can be nothing to do with Miss Hammond," said Annie. "She's in such a tizzy about the ball. And – and . . . she's one of those women who really only *talks*. I think perhaps she's a teensy bit mad."

"Of course Shaw-Bufford must be a very disappointed man," said the marquess.

"Why?"

"Well, if Mr. Macleod had been killed, then

Shaw-Bufford would have been the natural successor."

"Oh, I'm sure you are too hard on him," said Annie quickly. "He never struck me as being particularly ambitious."

"You're lying, my sweet," said her husband lazily.

"Don't be rude," snapped Annie. "By the way, what made you think the chancellor would ask me for money?"

"Because he needs a great deal of it in case he does not realize his ambition of becoming prime minister. It takes a lot of money to buy a peerage."

"But if he's ambitious and he's in the Commons, what can he possibly want with a peerage? It would be the end of his political career."

"In the Commons, yes. But what about the House of Lords?"

Annie shivered. "You make Mr. Shaw-Bufford sound quite sinister."

"How much did he ask you for?" came her husband's lazy voice.

"He didn't ask me for anything." Unfortunately, Annie, like most young girls who have been made to feel guilty all their young lives, was a spontaneous liar. She felt that she should never have agreed to give the chancellor money in the first place. She forgot that she had been ill and not in full possession of her wits at the time.

There was a silence. She was grateful that he could not see her face since the light from the carriage lamps was unable to penetrate the thickness of the fog. But, somehow, in the darkness, she fancied she could feel his brain searching hers, his sensitive antennae picking up her tension.

For one dreadful moment she sensed that he did not believe her, that he was about to say something.

But all he said was, "I wonder if we'll ever get there. This is the filthiest fog I can remember."

The fog became diffused with a yellow glare. They must be passing under the electric lights at Marble Arch. Then darkness descended again and the carriage began to move more rapidly.

Once again the marquess raised the trap.

"How is the going, John?" he called.

"Easier, my lord," came the coachman's voice over the rumble of the wheels. "Soon be there."

The Wintons' house was in Queens Gate. It was actually three houses knocked into one. The Wintons were very rich.

Fog had permeated the building so that despite the blazing fires, hundreds of candles, and banks of flowers, it was a bit like looking at a painting by Pissarro in reverse. Objects close up were distinct. A little distance away, however, and it was as if you were looking at them through gauze.

Two huge Indians in turbans waved enormous peacock fans back and forth at the entrance to the ballroom, but all their efforts did was to circulate the fog rather than to disperse it.

Annie had one dance with her husband, trying not to be seduced by thoughts of more intimate caresses conjured up by his nearness. For she had seen Harry Bellamy and was wondering how to make her move.

To her surprise, Harry Bellamy asked her for the next dance. He had been in the habit of dancing only with Marigold.

But after they had taken a few steps, his motives became clear. "Y'know," he said anxiously, "I felt the best thing, don't you know, was to ask you for a dance. Everyone's talking about that to-do in the park. 'Course I told them, I said, it's just a little tiff between sisters. Nothing to it, I said."

Annie turned a glowing face up to his. "Oh, Mr. Bellamy." She sighed. "How clever you are. How *diplomatic*! Marigold is such a lucky girl."

"Well, I say, that's dashed decent of you. I thought it was the right move m'self, but Marigold called me a fool."

"She must be joking," said Annie, bringing her long eyelashes into play. "No one could ever take you for a fool, Mr. Bellamy. *Oh!*"

"What's the matter?" said Harry Bellamy, anxiously, as Annie stumbled and clung to him.

"My ankle," said Annie, with a brave smile. "I twisted my ankle."

"I shall fetch your husband . . ."

"Oh, no, don't do that. If you could lead me to some anteroom where I could rest for a moment . . . I don't think it's too bad. And I would like an opportunity to ask your advice."

"I say," said Mr. Bellamy, fingering his moustache, "if you're sure it's all right . . ."

He placed an arm around her waist and led her from the ballroom. Marigold danced by with her partner and watched them leave, a look of shock on her face.

There was a small morning room on the ground floor, and it was there that Mr. Bellamy led Annie. He seemed to know the Wintons' house quite well.

Annie, who had not hurt her ankle at all, of

course, tried to remember to limp on the same foot but found herself alternating from the left to the right. As they reached the door of the morning room, Annie heard someone calling her name and bit her lip in vexation. Miss Mary Hammond came sailing up. Her large face looked very white.

"Have you seen Mr. Shaw-Bufford, Annie?" she panted.

"No, I have not," said Annie crossly. "If he is anywhere, it will be in the ballroom with the rest of the guests."

"I'll look again," said Miss Hammond. "Annie, I wonder if I could speak to you for a moment. I . . . well, I'm most awfully frightened and worried, and I don't know what to do."

Annie could not think of anyone as large as Miss Hammond being frightened. All she saw was an end to her plan to revenge on Marigold and her husband if she stayed to chat.

"I can't," she said. "Mary, I have wrenched my ankle and must rest it. Also I want to speak to Mr. Bellamy. I shall see you as soon as I can."

There was a step somewhere on the landing above, and Miss Hammond turned even whiter. She threw an anguished look at Annie, hesitated, and then hurried off.

"You know, I think that woman's mad," said Mr. Bellamy.

"Yes," agreed Annie, allowing him to lead her into the morning room.

Fog lay in long bands across the room. The air was musty and chilly.

They sat down on a small gilt sofa in front of the empty fireplace.

Annie, with well-feigned impulsiveness, took Mr. Bellamy's hands in her own and gazed intently up into his face while trying to think of a problem urgent enough to justify taking him away from the ballroom. All at once she thought she had it.

"I feel this ball is a sham, Mr. Bellamy," she said.

"Oh, I say," said Mr. Bellamy, fingering his waxed moustache.

"Yes. They say it's to raise funds for Women of the World, but it's really to raise funds for a society called Women's Rights, The Vote, and Feminine Equality."

"What! That's disgraceful," said Mr. Bellamy, roused to rare animation. "I say, the whole pack of 'em ought to be arrested. Particularly after nearly killing poor Macleod. Women get the vote. Ridiculous!"

Annie felt like striking him, felt like howling that there was absolutely nothing wrong in women getting a say in the running of the country, but instead she said meekly, "What should I do?"

She gazed up at him with shining eyes, leaning very close to him. She was wearing the perfume her husband had given her, being unable to keep the bottle stoppered any longer. Its exotic scent curled about Mr. Bellamy's pink ears. He looked down at her and grasped her hands more tightly, his rather prominent eyes beginning to bulge.

"Leave it to me," he said hoarsely. "I'll have a little word in Tommy Winton's ear. I mean, we shouldn't encourage these women. This could lead to anarchy. Anarchy! Little ladies like yourself should leave it to us strong men to handle things for you. You were very right to come to me. By Jove, I say, your eyes are awfully beautiful . . ."

He suddenly seized her in his arms and planted a wet kiss on her mouth just as the door opened.

The guilty couple released each other and swung around.

The marquess and Marigold stood on the threshold. The marquess looked calm and amused. But Marigold's eyes were wide with a mixture of fear and anger. She looked much younger than Annie at that moment, younger and lost and vulnerable. All at once, Annie realized how very badly she was behaving.

Marigold would have rushed forward, but the marquess held her back with a gentle hand on her arm.

"We were looking all over for you," he said lightly. "Your partners are languishing upstairs, my love."

"I – I sprained my ankle," said Annie wildly. "Mr. Bellamy brought me here so that I could rest it."

"How very kind of him," said the marquess. "But you really must not neglect your fiancée, Bellamy. My wife has me to look after her, you know. I shall have a little talk with you about that afterwards." Mr. Bellamy visibly cringed although the marquess's voice was as good-natured as ever. "Run along with Lady Marigold. You're missing all the fun."

For once Marigold was speechless. Harry Bellamy went over and took her arm, and she looked up at him with an odd, beseeching look.

The door closed behind them, leaving Annie and the marquess alone.

"We will give them a few moments to get back to the ballroom and then we will talk," said the marquess.

"I had better get back as well . . ."

"Oh, but you can't, my love. Not with your poor sprained ankle. Come with me!"

Annie opened her mouth to protest, shut it again, and took the arm he was holding out to her.

"I wish you would make up your mind which ankle it was you sprained," he said as he led her across the vast, deserted entrance hall. "You are limping on one foot and then the other."

"I think I sprained both," said Annie wretchedly, wondering why it was that one lie always led to a whole regiment of lies.

"I think you have sprained your brain. In here."

He pushed open the door of the Wintons' library. A fire was burning brightly in the hearth. Gaslight hissed quietly in the brackets over the mantel. Books that looked as if they had never been opened stood in serried ranks behind the glass fronts of the cases.

"Now," said her husband, turning to face her. His smiling mask had dropped and he looked very grim indeed. "Explain yourself!"

"I did," said Annie miserably. "I sprained my ankle . . . ankles . . . and Harry Bellamy took me away to rest a little. I saw nothing wrong in it. He is soon to be my brother-in-law."

"It seemed to me as if you were trying to make sure he would never be your brother-in-law but your lover instead."

"Why should you care?" Annie flashed back. "You and your fancy women!"

"Yes, me and my fancy women. Well, my dear, I manage not to disgrace you by kissing them in public. You simply got that poor sap, Bellamy, all roused up in order to make Marigold jealous. Is there no end to *your* jealousy? Or perhaps you would rather have married an idiot like Bellamy?"

"At least he would have been faithful to me."

"I think we should get one thing clear," said the marquess, coming to stand over her. "I, my dear, have certainly not led a celibate life. But I have at least been faithful to you since the day I married you."

"Pooh! Balderdash and tommyrot! What about the seductive Miss S.?"

"An old love. I met her in Paris and walked her down the Champs Elysées where I was photographed by a society photographer. We had an aperitif in a café and then I delivered her into the arms of her latest protector."

"And you expect me to believe that?"

He looked at her curiously. "Tell me, Annie," he asked, "are you so wrapped up in yourself that you never stop to think that other people have feelings, that other people get hurt? It's time you grew up and stopped behaving like a child thumbing her nose at adults. What you did this evening was childish and thoughtless and cruel."

"Nothing," said Annie, fiercely, "nothing I could ever do to you would be as cruel as your treatment of me. To go away and leave me alone for months. To cancel our honeymoon."

"A honeymoon is for lovers, Annie. It is not for a girl who has simply married me to compete with her sister."

"Will you *never* forget that?" said Annie bitterly.

"Make me." He stood looking down at her. "Make me, Annie. Make me forget your words."

She looked at him, trying to summon up the courage to take a step towards him, to throw herself into his arms and beg his forgiveness. She looked beyond him to the window, where the curtains were drawn back, trying to forget all the hurt.

The fog outside the window swirled in a rising wind. Through the curling, swirling fog, in the square of light cast on the garden outside by the gaslight in the room, a horrible, distorted, bloated face turned and danced.

It was much like one of the faces of the South Sea carvings back at Crammarth Castle with its mouth protruding from lips drawn back in a ghastly sort of grin.

Annie turned paper white.

She opened her mouth, but it was like one of those horrible dreams where you try to scream and no sound comes out, where you try to run, but your feet won't move.

The marquess turned around and looked at the window.

He gave a muttered exclamation and rang the bell by the fireplace.

"Sit down!" he said to Annie. "And put your head between your knees."

The door opened and a liveried footman came in.

The marquess waved his hand at the window. "There is a body out there, hanging," he said. "Be a good fellow and inform the police, the local hospital, and Mr. Winton, in that order."

The footman stared at the horror that was turning slowly outside the window. The thinning fog revealed that it was the body of Miss Hammond hanging from the rope.

From the open door came the laughter and chatter from the ballroom upstairs. The orchestra was playing a polka.

162

"Very good, my lord," said the footman.

"I never turned an 'air," he told the kitchen proudly afterwards. "I went up to Mr. Winton and I said: 'Sir,' I said, 'the Marquess of Torrance presents 'is compliments and says to tell you that there is a body a-hanging from a rope outside the 'ouse. I have informed the Yard, sir, as per 'is lordship's instructions.' "

"Come along," said the marquess to Annie. "What a bloody, sickening sort of evening. The police will know where to find me if they want me."

Annie silently allowed him to help her out of the house. She could not get the memory of that dreadful face out of her mind. Somewhere at the back of her mind was a growing fear. Somewhere, somehow, someone had said something. She knew something quite dreadful and yet she could not think of what it was.

The silence of her rooms at home weighed down on her. After Barton had made her mistress ready for bed, Annie sat in front of her dressing table, brushing her long red hair with automatic strokes of the brush. Barton had told her in a hushed whisper that two gentlemen from Scotland Yard had called to see the master.

The little gilt clock on the mantel chimed a silvery two in the morning.

The door opened and her husband stood there. His face was set in harsh, stern lines as he studied her reflection in the glass.

"They've gone," he said curtly. "Go to bed."

Now was the time to say she was sorry, but a dreadful, stubborn pride held her back.

Almost as if he knew what was going through her head, he said, "Oh, go to bed and dream of ruining Marigold's life – and pray for the wisdom to realize you are ruining your own."

The door slammed. Annie stared miserably at her reflection. Why did she always feel like a naughty child? Couldn't he understand? He ought to *know*.

"But he's not psychic," said the cynical voice of her conscience. "And he'll never know unless you tell him."

But it was too late, tonight anyway, thought cowardly Annie. And – and she had seen a dead body. And – and he should have realized her feminine feelings were lacerated and have been proud of her, yes *proud*. For she had not screamed or fainted.

All at once, she remembered the feel of Harry Bellamy's soft, hot mouth and writhed with shame. Then there was that lost, hurt look in Marigold's eyes.

Oh, why couldn't life be black and white?

Annie trailed miserably to bed.

But sleep would not come.

Every time she closed her eyes, the bloated, dead face of Miss Hammond rose before her inner vision.

Like a sleepwalker, Annie swung her legs out of bed and walked slowly out of her room and along to her husband's door. She gave the door a jerk to open it and went inside.

Light was shining from the bedroom beyond his sitting room. Annie hesitated, longing to turn back and yet frightened of the nightmares that lay in wait for her, frightened of her own guilty conscience.

He was lying propped up on the pillows reading a book. As she entered, he put the book down on the covers and looked at her, his face rigid, his eyes cold.

Annie couldn't help remembering his former lazy good humor, his smiling eyes, as she looked at the stern, handsome face against the whiteness of the pillows.

"What is it?" he said.

"I'm frightened," whispered Annie.

"No doubt," he said in a flat voice. "It is not every day one sees a dead body. I suggest you

165

wake Barton and ask her to sleep in your room for the night."

Annie dimly realized that he must have once had some feeling, some affection for her. Why else would she now notice the sudden lack of it?

"I want to sleep with you," said Annie, trembling with the cold and nerves.

"Very well. So long as you don't mind if I go on reading."

Annie removed her dressing gown and placed it on a chair. She was wearing a white satin nightgown chosen for her by her mother. It covered more of her body than a ball gown. She walked around to the far side of the bed and pulled back the covers, noticing before she climbed in that her husband was naked.

She pulled the blankets up and lay very still. But she found that she had exchanged one sort of agony for another. She could feel the heat emanating from his body a few inches away from her own. Her whole being started to throb and ache for his touch. Her treacherous body started to shake and tremble.

"If you are cold," he said, without raising his eyes from the page, "I will fetch some more blankets."

"It's not that," said Annie miserably. "It's . . ." At a loss for words, she turned on

166

her side to face him and put one small, cold, trembling hand on his chest.

He twisted his head and looked at her. Her eyes were wide and pleading and bright with unshed tears. Her soft mouth trembled.

"Bloody, *bloody* hell!" said the marquess savagely. He threw his book on the floor and jerked the bedclothes down to the foot of the bed.

"Take off that repellent thing you're wearing," he commanded.

"Put out the light," pleaded Annie. The room was lit by the soft glow of one oil lamp on the marquess's side of the bed.

"No. I said, take it off."

Blushing, Annie pulled her nightdress over her head.

"Now," said the Marquess of Torrance. "Come here and kiss me."

Annie threw herself on his chest and kissed him inexpertly on the mouth.

He gathered her into his arms and rolled over so that he was lying on top of her, propped up on his elbows.

"Do you want me to make love to you?" he demanded.

"Yes, Jasper," whispered Annie shyly.

"Do you want me?"

"Yes."

"How much?" he said. "Tell me how much!"

"Very much," she said in such a low voice that he had to strain his ears to hear.

Then his eyes gleamed with laughter. He lowered himself down on top of her, the hard weight of his chest pressing against her breasts. "Prepare for a long night, my lady." He grinned. "Let's spend our first passion quickly so that I may explore this delicious body of yours at my leisure. I will stop only when I have discovered that your passion matches your temper."

After the first violent lovemaking was over, Annie felt so exhausted that she thought she would sleep forever. But his lips were moving down her body and every nerve leaped in response until she buried her hands in his thick hair and cried to him to take her again. As the pale dawn light filtered into the room, Annie looked up into her husband's eyes and saw that they were filled with tenderness and a sort of amazed gratitude.

Her last waking thought was that for the first time in her life she had done something right.

His caressing hands woke her some hours later. The birds were singing outside, and the noises of the street came to their ears.

But, for Annie, all worries and fears had gone. All of the busy world had gone away. All of the universe was reduced to the touch of his lips and the feel of his long fingers, stroking her and turning her from one delicious position to another.

Mary Hammond, Mr. Shaw-Bufford, Marigold, and Harry Bellamy whirled and turned and disappeared from her mind as the Marchioness of Torrance proved over and over again that her passion could outmatch her temper.

Annie floated downstairs sometime in mid-afternoon, dressed and ready to face what was left of the day. She had retired to her own rooms to bathe and change after the long and exhausting night and morning in her husband's arms.

A servant had told her that the marquess wished to see her downstairs as soon as she was ready.

A small smile curved Annie's bruised mouth. He had not said he loved her during their exquisite, shared passion. Now she was sure he would.

She was therefore startled to find her husband waiting for her at the foot of the stairs with a grim look on his face.

Annie tilted her face up for a kiss and closed her eyes.

He seemed not to notice, for when she opened them again he was half turned away from her and saying, "Those two chaps from Scotland Yard are back. I put them in the study. They want to speak to you."

All of Annie's newfound esteem crumbled away. She did not care who was waiting for her in the study. All she cared about was that he had not kissed her. He did not care for her. Last night meant nothing to him. It did not dawn on her for a moment that her husband was very worried about something and had not even noticed her offered kiss.

"Well, if they've come to see me, I suppose I'd better see them," she said in a brittle voice, sweeping in front of him toward the study.

Two middle-aged men rose at her entrance. Her husband followed her in and closed the door. "May I present Detective Inspectors Carton and Johns of the Yard. Mr. Carton, Mr. Johns, my wife."

Annie gave them a chilly nod and took a seat facing them. The marquess stood behind her chair.

Mr. Carton was the spokesman. He was not like Annie's idea of a policeman at all. He was very tall and distinguished-looking with a thin, intelligent face.

"We wish to ask you a few questions, my lady," he began. "It concerns the death of Miss Hammond."

Annie flushed guiltily. Suddenly it seemed terrible that she had not given one thought since last night to that poor woman's death.

I found Miss Hammond a trifle eccentric," she said hesitantly. "But I would not have said she was the sort of lady to take her own life."

"Exactly," said Mr. Carton, in a level voice.

"But she seemed very worried . . . almost frightened . . . when I last saw her. Oh, dear!" Annie blushed miserably again. She remembered the look on Mary Hammond's white face and how she had turned even whiter at the sound of a step on the landing above.

"You have remembered something," prompted Mr. Carton gently.

"Yes, I . . ." Annie twisted her head and looked up anxiously at her husband.

His face wore a closed, shuttered look as he stared straight in front of him.

"Yes?" Mr. Carton prompted again.

"Well, it was at the ball. She said she wanted to speak to me about something."

"And did she?"

"Well, no. You see, I was talking to my

future brother-in-law, Mr. Harry Bellamy, so I said I'd see her later. Oh, she asked me if I had seen Mr. Shaw-Bufford."

"I gather Mr. Shaw-Bufford arrived after the body of Miss Hammond had been found."

"Perhaps," said Annie miserably, "if I had given her the time, if only I had spoken to her, she would not have done this terrible thing."

"You are under the impression that Miss Hammond committed suicide?"

Annie stared at the inspector, wide-eyed. "But of course she did. You can't mean . . .?"

"It was made to look like suicide, yes, but in fact Miss Hammond was murdered. The autopsy was performed this morning and it revealed that Miss Hammond had been strangled by someone *before* the rope was put around her neck."

"Oh," said Annie weakly. Everything suddenly seemed unreal: the two detectives sitting so solemnly across from her, her husband standing rigidly behind her, the ticking of the black marble clock above the fireplace.

"We also found evidence in Miss Hammond's lodgings that points to the fact that she may well have been the lady who tried to kill the prime minister yesterday. She bungled the job, so someone killed her. A powerful woman could do the job."

Annie began to feel sick.

"So," pursued Mr. Carton, "we want you to tell us about this society. Miss Hammond gave lectures, that we know. But she had no record of having undertaken any militant action before. We would have said she simply enjoyed public speaking. Can you think of any members of her society who might have killed her?"

Annie shook her head. "It's silly, but I never really got to know any of them. She was a sort of one-woman organization when I first met her at Britlingsea. Then she called and asked if she could use this house for a committee meeting. I agreed. I knew some of the women who came, certainly Mrs. Tommy Winton, who gave the ball, and some of the other society ladies. But the ones I knew, well, I think they were simply using the whole thing as an excuse to have a sort of charity ball.

"The other women – there were about three – who seemed to belong to Miss Hammond's new movement, I hadn't seen them before, and I doubt if I would recognize any of them again."

"Were the speeches – I assume there were speeches – particularly militant? Was there any mention of Mr. Macleod's name?"

Annie passed a hand over her brow. "I can't

remember. I was coming down with influenza and I was already running a fever, you see, and I was out of the room most of the time Miss Hammond was talking."

"Where did you go? To lie down?"

"N-no. Mr. Shaw-Bufford wanted to talk to me – in the study."

Mr. Carton leaned forward. "What did he want to see you about, my lady?"

Annie stared at the floor.

"My lady," said Mr. Carton, "this is a murder investigation. You must tell me why the chancellor wished to talk to you in private."

"He wanted to ask me for money," mumbled Annie.

She could almost feel her husband's hands tightening on the back of the chair. She had lied to him. She had told him that Mr. Shaw-Bufford had not asked her for money.

"For himself?"

"No. For Miss Hammond's society."

"How much, my lady?"

"T-ten thousand pounds."

"Ten *thousand* pounds! That's a great deal of money. A fortune!"

"I didn't give it to him," said Annie quickly.

"And that was the end of the matter?"

There was a long silence. The fog had

cleared, but a dismal, gusty, blustery wind was howling through the streets of London. A torn newspaper danced an erratic ballet in front of the window. The window frame rattled. The fire crackled and the clock ticked.

"My lady," said Mr. Carton, "the only way we are going to solve this business is by demanding complete honesty from all the people we have to interview. Now, I will repeat my question. Did the chancellor just let the matter drop?"

Oh, thought Annie, miserably, Jasper is going to find out how I have lied and lied again.

"I felt ill. I needed time," she said wearily. "I told him to come back on Wednesday. He did. But I was too ill to see him. When I finally did see him, I said I would make out the check to the society. My husband had told me to do that. He said I was never to make a check out to an individual. Mr. Shaw-Bufford was . . . well, rather insistent. So I told him I had no money of my own. I lied. I said that he should ask my husband. And he left. He – he was angry."

"Well, then, my lady," said Mr. Carton. "Don't distress yourself. We shall probably find that Mr. Shaw-Bufford wanted the money for the society and for no other reason. Now, is there anything else you can think of that might help us?"

There was. Annie was sure there was something there at the back of her mind, but, for the life of her, she couldn't think of what it was.

She shook her head dumbly.

"I may as well tell you, my lady, that I spoke to Mr. Harry Bellamy this morning. He said that you were worried about the ball being a sham. That it was not really for something vague like Women of the World, but for a feminist society run by Miss Hammond. In fact, he called in person at the Yard to tell us. Were you, in fact, very upset by this deception?"

Poor Annie felt that she had told enough truth for one morning.

"Yes," she said.

"I am afraid that was not the case," came the voice of her husband from behind her. "My wife pretended to sprain her ankle so as to manufacture an opportunity of being alone with Mr. Bellamy. I think you will find that my wife doesn't care two pins whether women get the vote or not. She merely wanted to make her sister jealous. Lady Marigold Sinclair is affianced to Mr. Bellamy."

"Is this true, my lady?" asked Mr. Carton.

176

"Yes," said Annie, in a stifled voice. In that moment she could have killed her husband. How *dare* he hold her actions up to ridicule?

"Then I think that will be all for the moment," said the inspector, signaling to his colleague. "I hope I do not have to trouble you again. My lord, my lady, good day to you."

After the policemen had left, Annie walked to the window and stared out at the dismal day.

"I hope you're satisfied," she said in a low voice.

"Yes," came her husband's infuriatingly bland voice. "It was necessary to tell the police the truth. That way you cannot be suspected of murder."

"Don't be silly," said Annie, whirling around to face him.

"It also cleared the air. There has been too much misunderstanding between us. I ask you not to lie to me again, Annie."

"You pompous ass," howled Annie. "How dare you stand there and pontificate? How dare you tell those coppers that I have no interest in women getting the vote? I care very much. I think women have a damn hard time of it. I think *I* have a hard time of it being married to you."

"On the contrary, you have a very easy

time. You are very much your own mistress. You came to me willingly last night, or do I have to remind you of that?"

"That was because I was afraid," Annie flashed back. "I had just seen a dead body for the first time in my life, and a pretty awful one at that!"

"And what went on between us last night? How do you interpret that, my fair lady?"

"Lust!"

Although he did not move an inch, it was as if he were retreating from her, step by step, moving away, moving far away to the other side of a great, black gulf of resentment and hurt and misunderstanding.

The silence seemed to go on forever.

Then he gave a little shrug. "I have business to attend to," said the Marquess of Torrance.

And so he left.

Annie had never felt more alone in her life.

Chapter Seven

ANNIE sat in front of the Houses of Parliament, surrounded by ranks of silent women, all demanding the vote with their long vigil.

The only comfort she had was the realization that she was doing it because she really thought women should get the vote and not to revenge herself on her husband.

During the past few weeks, she had hardly seen him at all, and when she had he had been polite and punctilious. At that moment, he was in the House of Lords. He had been up most of the night before preparing his speech. That much Annie had gleaned from the servants, who were most impressed that his lordship wrote his own speeches and did not employ the services of a secretary.

Annie had, however, seen quite a deal of Detective-Inspector Carton. He had returned on one occasion, bringing with him Chief Superintendent Delaney who, he said, was in charge of the case.

The chief superintendent was a large, fatherly man who quickly put Annie at her ease. He took her over the whole business again, starting with her first meeting with Miss Hammond.

Mr. Shaw-Bufford had appeared as a genuine champion of women's rights, Mr. Delaney had said. Annie wondered whether to pass on her husband's cynical opinion that the chancellor wanted to buy a peerage but decided against it.

Miss Hammond, it transpired, had been a country solicitor's daughter, living on a small annuity left her in her parents' will. Her lodgings in Bayswater had been depressingly shabby, Mr. Delaney had said. A rifle, recently fired, had been found hidden under the mattress, together with a diary that left very little doubt in the minds of the police that Miss Hammond had been guilty of the attempt on the life of the prime minister.

"He tells me it is the only way," Miss Hammond had written after describing how she meant to go about shooting Mr. Macleod outside the House of Commons. "I trust him because he is wise, although some call him Evil."

Annie shivered and pulled her cloak more tightly about her shoulders. The "he" of the diary, Mr. Delaney had decided, was probably the devil. He had asked if Miss Hammond had shown any signs of being a religious fanatic, but Annie had said that Miss Hammond only appeared fanatical on the subject of men.

The women who surrounded Annie during the vigil were mostly well-to-do, middle-class women. Annie had been sitting there for seven hours and she was feeling chilled to the bone. But if they could do it, she could, she told herself sternly. She had decided to wait until the House rose in three hours' time, then go home and have a hot bath.

Several times she had thought of going to her husband and explaining what had driven her to say those things. That it was not just because he had made her feel like a fool in front of the police; it was because he seemed to have joined the serried ranks of authority figures who always made her feel like a fool.

Her mother and father were in London to begin the preparations for Marigold's wedding. The countess had called on Annie to exclaim with horror over the fact that her younger daughter had got her name involved in a murder scandal. How Annie had longed to unburden herself. To cry for advice! But her mother had seemed as chilly and aloof as ever and was completely taken up with relishing the idea of what a beautiful bride Marigold would make.

Annie had then called on Mrs. Tommy Winton, hoping that that lady might have some advice on the difficulties of marriage.

But it seemed that Mrs. Winton and her society friends in some way blamed Annie for the ruin of their ball. Annie should have known, Mrs. Winton had said, rattling the teacups, that Mary Hammond was the sort of woman to do a terribly embarrassing thing like hanging herself in the most public manner possible.

Annie had tried to point out that it was a case of murder, not suicide, to which Mrs. Winton had replied with a superior smile that it was just like Annie to side with the police. She had added insult to injury by saying that she had decided that the whole idea of the vote for women was quite ridiculous and rather distasteful. Much better to leave the running of the country to the men. Equality was ridiculous. Had women had to fight the Boers? No, of course not. Well, if Annie and her ilk pursued their mad course, they would end up on the battlefield, fighting alongside the men and absolutely ruining their complexions. Although mud *was* said to be beneficial. Had Annie heard of the latest treatment at Solange? It was at this point that Annie had left.

And so Annie was left feeling more than ever like a child adrift in an incomprehensible adult world.

She longed to apologize to her husband. But she was terrified that he would reject her apology. And her stubborn pride kept telling her that he should be the one to apologize first.

Annie had met Marigold and her fiancé at the opera three nights ago. Harry Bellamy had twirled his moustache and leered at her, and

Marigold had looked angry and hurt.

The minutes dragged by. Now she realized why some women preferred more militant action. At times anything seemed preferable to this long, silent war.

All at once she remembered the laughing tenderness in her husband's eyes after they had made love. Surely that was love! Did one have to say it? Had he not shown her that he loved her, that it was more than lust?

Annie clenched her frozen hands in her lap. This evening, this very evening, she would apologize to him. And, having made that decision, she felt as if a great weight had been lifted from her shoulders.

Rain started pattering down on her felt hat, a few little drops, then more, then a steady downpour. She was glad that she had had the foresight to bring her umbrella and broke her silence by offering to share its shelter with the woman next to her.

"Thank you very much," said her companion, briskly. "I was so sure it wouldn't rain. I hope I don't catch a cold because my husband will really be angry with me. He told me it would rain."

"I suppose it's all right if we talk," ventured Annie. "I know it's supposed to be a silent vigil . . ."

"Well, nobody will hear us in this deluge. I think we ought to stand up, don't you? Our skirts will be soaked in no time."

"No one else is standing up," said Annie, looking around.

"Oh, well." Her companion sighed. "I suppose we should all stick together."

"I'm Annie Torrance," said Annie, feeling an introduction was necessary.

"Very pleased to meet you. I'm Agnes Merriweather. Did you say Torrance? You're not the Marchioness of Torrance?"

Annie nodded.

"Oh, your poor thing! I saw your name in the papers, my lady. I was reading about that Hammond business. We're all mystified. If she had been a member of a large militant group – you know, the kind who smash windows in Oxford Street and snipe at passing trains – I could have understood it. But no one in any of the feminist movements had ever really heard of her. She was a member of the Women's National and Political Union at one time, I believe, but she didn't make any friends. Who do you think would kill her?"

"I don't know," said Annie. "I keep thinking it must have been a woman. But perhaps it was one of the men who got so infuriated with all she stood for."

"But she didn't really stand for anything but herself," protested Mrs. Merriweather. "I gather she made vague sorts of speeches, all down with men and that sort of thing, traveling around the country and speaking in damp church halls to tiny audiences of bored women."

"I first met her at Britlingsea," said Annie. "She had some idea that we should cease all intimacy with men until we got what we wanted."

Mrs. Merriweather laughed. "What woman in her right mind wants to do that? You don't think some woman took her seriously and her husband strangled Mary Hammond in revenge? Of course, any woman who does that ought to end up in the divorce courts."

Annie flushed. "Or man," she said.

Mrs. Merriweather shifted a large handbag to her other arm and stole a look at her companion's face.

"Forgive me, my lady," she said. "But you look very unhappy. Is this business of Miss Hammond's murder preying on your mind?"

"That . . . and – and other things. I need a woman to talk to."

"I'm one. We're not acquainted, but sometimes it's easier to talk to a stranger."

It was Annie's turn to study her

companion's face. Mrs. Merriweather was middle-aged, with gray hair peeping out from under the brim of her hat. She had round, red cheeks and rather pleasant, faded blue eyes.

"It's this," Annie burst out. "I'm not on speaking terms with my husband."

"And you married so recently! Perhaps he does not approve of what you are doing. Oh, how silly. Of course he must. That was a splendid speech he made in the Lords about women's rights."

Annie turned a dull red. "I didn't know," she faltered. "Nobody told me . . ."

"Well, it was in all the newspapers. He came under a lot of fire, but then he's so witty his adversaries were left standing. But that's not the problem between you?"

"No," said Annie. "Look, I'm going to tell you about it. I must get advice from some-one . . ."

And so Annie proceeded to unburden herself, feeling as she did so that she was breaking some rigid social code. Men, she knew, did not discuss their wives. Perhaps that was why so many of them died of high-blood pressure.

Mrs. Merriweather listened in attentive silence.

When Annie was finished, she said gently, "He must be very much in love with you."

"But he never *said* so."

"You don't go by what people *say* but by what they *do*. There are some happy marriages, where, I am sure, the word love has never been mentioned. If Lord Torrance had not been in love with you, then he would not have been so hurt when you told him you had only married him to get revenge on your sister."

"Perhaps that was just hurt pride," said Annie. "My pride gets dreadfully hurt."

"Now you move in a much more elevated society that I, my lady," said Mrs. Merriweather. "But the social columns can't *all* be wrong. I was under the impression that the Marquess of Torrance could have married anyone he wanted to."

Annie nodded.

"But he didn't. He married you. And very quickly, too."

"That – that could have been to get my money," said Annie, who had already told her companion of the legacy.

"But your husband is one of the richest men in the country! Didn't you know that? His wealth is legendary, and that home of his, Frileton House, is a palace!"

"I didn't know," said Annie. "But," she burst out, "if there is to be equality in a marriage, surely *he* should apologize to *me*."

"Well, it seems he was in the wrong, too. But I think he has the advantage over you. *He* married you for love. Also, if you think enough of yourself, there's nothing wrong with apologizing. If you don't learn to do that, then marital rows can go on for weeks. It's no use thinking the whole time that your husband is being nasty to you just because he *is* nasty. Goodness, how wet we're getting! All this rainwater. My boots feel like swimming baths. Not long to go now. I'll tell you a story to pass the time." Mrs. Merriweather poked a strand of gray hair under her hat and adjusted her heavy handbag.

"Now Albert, my husband, was very moody when I started going on these vigils. Every time I came home, he was more angry and crusty than the day before. I naturally assumed, therefore, that he was like most men and thought all this feminist business was a farce, and so, as he became angrier, I became more silent and bitter, and by the end of one week we weren't speaking to each other *at all.*

"But somehow I suddenly found myself thinking, this is silly. So I simply went and asked him what the matter was, and he told me he thought I hadn't been sitting outside the House of Commons, but that I was meeting some fellow on the sly. Well, I was very tempted to laugh because it's very flattering when you come to think of it, considering my age and the fact that we've been married twenty years! It sounds funny now, but it was nearly the end of our marriage before I explained things. Lack of communication is a dreadful thing."

"I had already made up my mind to apologize," said Annie shyly. "I think I'll find it a lot easier after talking to you."

At last the House rose, and so did Annie and her companion. They were soaked to the skin, and Annie was shivering so much her teeth rattled. She said good-bye to Mrs. Merriweather.

Neither woman thought of exchanging addresses or of arranging to see each other again. For Annie was of the aristocracy and Mrs. Merriweather was middle-class and lived in Camberwell. Later in life this would strike Annie as very strange and she would often find herself thinking of Mrs. Merriweather. But, for the moment, the vote for women was revolutionary enough and left little space in Annie's mind for any thoughts of breaking down the English caste system, or, indeed, of questioning it all.

She did, however, feel a pleasurable sensation of guilt to have a mansion full of servants to return to, to have her bath drawn and scented with rose water, to have her clothes laid out for her. She hoped the rest of the women who had been on the vigil were half as lucky.

"Tell my husband I shall join him in half an hour," Annie called to the maid, Barton, who was arranging jars and bottles on the toilet table. "We are going to the Bunburys' tonight."

"My lord has already left," came Barton's voice. "It's ten o'clock, my lady. He thought you did not have any intention of going."

Annie appeared from the bathroom, wrapped in a fleecy towel, and stared at the clock in dismay. It had been a late-night sitting in the House and she had been so absorbed in listening to Mrs. Merriweather that she had not noticed the passage of time.

"Then I will follow him," she said. "Tell Perkins to have the carriage brought around in half an hour."

Annie stood at the entrance to the Bunburys' ballroom, feeling as shy and as gauche as she had done a few months ago. Her gown of lilac silk had a corsetlike, close-fitting bodice with a round waist. The décolletage was low and off the shoulder with large, "balloon" short sleeves. The skirt had a train and lace-trimmed side panels.

Her red hair was brushed back off her forehead in a simpler style than she usually affected.

Mr. and Mrs. Bunbury were a bright young couple who adored giving balls and parties, and their mansion in Kensington always seemed to be full of guests. They had long ago left their stance at the top of the stairs to join the ball. Couples whirled around in the inevitable waltz. There was Marigold, looking enchanting in sky-blue silk and lace, in the arms of Harry Bellamy. And among the chaperones was Aunt Agatha, painted like a mask. Mr. Shaw-Bufford was dancing with Mrs. Tommy Winton. He saw Annie and bent his head to whisper something in Mrs. Winton's ear, and Mrs. Winton threw back her head and laughed.

After some hesitation, and being unable to see her husband, Annie walked around the edge of the floor and took a seat beside Aunt Agatha.

Aunt Agatha promptly unfurled her large, ostrich feather fan and proceeded to grumble behind it.

"It quite ruins my evening to see you here, Annie," she said. "Poor Marigold's nerves were in *shreds* after that terrible scene in the park. Miss Higgins and old Nanny Simpkins are in town for the wedding – dear Marigold is always so considerate and had invited all the old servants from Scotland – and they tell me that you have always been terribly jealous of Marigold. I thought your silly behaviour would have ceased when you married Torrance, for after all he *is* a marquess and a better catch than Bellamy. But no! You simply had to pick on the poor girl . . ."

"Aunt Agatha," said Annie, grimly. "Cease this tirade immediately. I behaved badly, but the provocation was great. But I am a married lady at a ball. I am not a girl in the schoolroom. Now, where is my husband?"

"Torrance? Probably still in the supper room. But I must warn you . . ."

But Annie had left.

It was eleven-thirty. Supper had been served at nine-thirty, which was very early, but the Bunburys were proud of their French chef and liked to make sure that all of their guests were fed, even the dowagers who did not like to stay all night.

The supper room was nearly empty. A few couples were still seated at small tables shaded by lamps. In the far corner, by the window, sat her husband. He was entertaining a diminutive blonde who was laughing with delight at everything he said. Annie's hands in their suede evening gloves clenched and unclenched.

He was wearing a new evening suit: a dress coat with a plain collar and silk-covered revers, worn over a white waistcoat, and long, narrow trousers trimmed down the side of each leg with braid.

He looked debonair, relaxed. He looked as if he hadn't a care in the world.

He looked as if he hadn't a wife.

Annie moved forward and put a hand on the back of his chair. The pretty blonde was telling him about some musical comedy she had just seen and did not even look up. The marquess did not turn around although Annie could have sworn that he was aware of her presence.

"Jasper," she said, hoping her voice was not as shrill as it sounded to her own ears.

Then he turned around, smiled, and got to his feet.

"I'm sorry I'm late," said Annie.

"Don't worry," said her husband. "I have been well entertained. Allow me to present Mrs. Freddie Bangor. Mrs. Bangor, my wife."

"Delighted to make your acquaintance," said Mrs. Bangor, flashing a smile that started somewhere in Annie's direction and ended up in the marquess's. "My husband couldn't come this evening, so dear Jasper and I were consoling each other."

"Well, you don't need to do that any longer now that I am here," said Annie sweetly. "I see you have finished your meal, Mrs. Bangor, and I do want a word in private with my husband, so . . ."

"But there is plenty of room at the table for three," said her husband, with maddening good humor. "I am sure whatever it is can wait." He pulled a chair forward between himself and Mrs. Bangor. Annie reluctantly sat down. The marquess signaled to a footman and ordered supper for Annie.

"Now, Dolly," he said to Mrs. Bangor, "do go on. It sounds quite a fascinating plot."

"Well, it was fun, really," said Mrs. Bangor. Her eyelashes were quite definitely false, Annie thought sourly. "You see, it turned out she wasn't a simple village girl after all, but a Russian princess. Fancy! So of course it was all right for the prince to marry her. Oh, it was so moving. They hold hands and sing 'Our Love Will Last Forever.' How does it go? Let me see . . . tum-titty, tum-titty, tum, tum, tum."

"Not a very good lyric," said Annie nastily.

"Well, it's not the *words*, dear. It's the

tune," explained Mrs. Bangor, as if talking to an idiot.

"You must forgive my wife," said the marquess blandly. "Annie is quite tone deaf, you know. More salad, my dear?"

"I am *not* tone deaf, Jasper, and I do not want any salad. I want . . ."

"Oh, here's Lady Marigold. And Harry! Well, that's splendid," said the marquess, getting to his feet. "Marigold and I have the next dance, Annie. Harry, be a good chap and sit with my wife. You know Mrs. Bangor, of course. Dolly, do tell Mr. Bellamy about that simply splendid musical. . . ."

He walked off with Marigold, who threw a mocking look at Annie over her shoulder.

Annie sat and fumed. She was very hungry, but she thought that the food would choke her.

Mrs. Bangor had started to tell them all about the musical from the opening scene to the grand finale. At last Annie felt that she could bear it no longer. She muttered an excuse and left the table.

As soon as Annie entered the ballroom, she was accosted by her hosts and had to stand and chat with them for several moments, while all the time she was aware of her husband with Marigold in his arms, dipping and swaying and pirouetting.

"They make a handsome couple," said little Mrs. Bunbury, and then she giggled. "Oh, I say, I quite forgot he was your husband!"

Annie's head felt hot and heavy, and she realized she had caught a chill.

And then Mr. Shaw-Bufford was at her side, begging for the next dance.

"I don't feel like dancing," said Annie, looking at the chancellor with some distaste. "In fact, I think I have caught another cold, Mr. Shaw-Bufford, and I would rather sit down."

"But, of course," he said, smiling. "What about some cold champagne? An excellent remedy."

Annie nodded weakly and allowed him to lead her back to the supper room. She did not want to be in his company, but, on the other hand, she did not want to stand at the edge of the ballroom watching her husband flirting.

Mr. Shaw-Bufford found her a secluded table in a corner far away from where Mrs. Bangor was still entertaining Harry Bellamy.

After two ice-cold glasses of champagne, Annie began to feel quite warm towards the chancellor. He had talked easily and pleasantly of this and that. He had told her that she was looking very beautiful, and that was balm to

Annie's wounded esteem. And Scotland Yard had said that he was genuine in his support of the feminist movement.

Suddenly she realized that his voice had taken on a more serious tone and he was saying, "Well, I gather we are no longer considered murderers by the gentlemen of the Yard."

"Murderers!" squeaked Annie. "They couldn't have possibly considered me a murderer."

"They had found out about your fight in the park with your sister, and I think they considered that, were you in a rage, you might have exceptional strength."

"But that's ridiculous. Did you say they suspected you? But surely your high position should—"

"Protect me? Alas, no. That was what gave me the motive in their eyes. You see, with Jimmy Macleod gone, I would then be in line for prime minister. They may have wondered if I had put Miss Hammond up to the shooting, and, when she failed, well, I simply got rid of her. Fortunately for me, I was in my club at the time the murder was taking place."

Annie shivered and sneezed. "I often wonder who did it," she said.

"Oh, some fanatic. Let me fill your glass."

"I also wonder about poor Miss Hammond. What drove her to take such a crazy action? I suppose there is no hope it was really suicide?"

"Well, of course, I think it was," said the chancellor. "I feel the police have bungled and are too pigheaded to admit their error. Some women are born to be martyrs, and Mary Hammond was one of them."

Annie sat very still. Her head was hot, and the room was becoming blurred. She had a sudden flash of total recall. The supper room spun away and she was back again outside the study door, listening to the voices of the chancellor and Mary Hammond.

"If I am caught, I shall at least be a martyr . . ."

"You will not be caught, Miss Hammond. Remember, my name must never be mentioned. Never!"

Gradually she returned to reality. The chancellor was looking at her oddly. Mrs. Bangor over at the other end of the room had reached her favorite song. "Tum-titty, tum-titty, tum, tum, tum," she sang.

"Jolly good that, what!" Harry Bellamy chortled.

"Are you ill?" Mr. Shaw-Bufford was leaning forward, looking at Annie intently.

"What," said Annie, "did you mean, Mr.

Shaw-Bufford, when you told Miss Hammond that she would never be caught – and that your name must never be mentioned? It was after she said that at least she would be a martyr if she were caught."

"I am sure I said nothing of the kind," said the chancellor smoothly. "Your glass is empty, Lady Torrance. A little more?"

"But you *did*," said Annie fretfully. "I heard you. I was outside the study door when you were talking."

"You misunderstood," said Mr. Shaw-Bufford. "I hope you didn't tell any of this nonsense to the police?"

"I couldn't," said Annie simply. "I've only just remembered. Mr. Carton is calling tomorrow to see if I can remember anything more."

"You must not trouble him with things you only think you heard."

"Oh, but I did hear it," said Annie wearily. "I won't tell him what you said. Just the bit about Miss Hammond expecting to be a martyr. They might find that important."

Mr. Shaw-Bufford took a deep breath. "You must do as you see fit. You look unwell, Lady Torrance. Perhaps I should fetch your husband."

"Please," Annie said in a small voice. She now felt very ill. She knew vaguely that she had said something she should not.

The chancellor stood up. He seemed to loom over her. "Lady Torrance," he began urgently. Then he gave a shrug and was gone.

After a few moments he was back. He pulled his chair close to Annie's and took her hand in his.

"I am afraid your husband is otherwise occupied," he said in a low voice.

"What?" asked Annie, dizzy from the effects of the champagne and a rising temperature. "What do you mean?"

"I hate to see a lady such as you – a lady I have come to care for deeply – being so deceived. Your husband was not in the ballroom. I questioned the servants and found him in a small room leading off the ballroom at the far end. He had your sister in his arms and he was kissing her – passionately."

Annie's world fell apart. Gone was the Marchioness of Torrance. In her place sat little Annie Sinclair, humiliated again.

"Take me home," she said through dry lips.

"Certainly," he said in a low voice. "We will leave through that door at the other end. That way we will avoid attracting notice."

Blindly, Annie let him lead her away down a back staircase, out of a side entrance, and into his waiting carriage.

Ill as she was, it dawned on Annie after a time that surely they should have been turning into St. James's Square by now. She looked out of the carriage window and recognized Trafalgar Square.

"Where are we going?" asked Annie.

"I have left some important papers at my flat," said the chancellor. "I must pick them up and then I will take you home."

"Wouldn't it have been more sensible to have dropped me off first?" said Annie, shivering and sneezing.

"You are right. Forgive me," he said. "I was so concerned about the papers that I did not think. It will only take me a moment, and my man can give you something for your cold."

"Oh, very well," said Annie. "Only make it quick." All she wanted to do was to sink in between nice, cool sheets and go to sleep, shutting away all the misery and hurt.

How could she have ever believed that she could have attracted the catch of the Season? Yet why did he marry her? Why? Why? Why?

The carriage lurched to a stop. Had she not felt so ill, Annie would never have dreamed of entering any man's lodgings without a chaperone.

The chancellor's flat was in a quiet street in

the shadow of the Houses of Parliament. Big Ben chimed one o'clock, a long, slow note like a death knell.

"Ah, Hodder," said Mr. Shaw-Bufford, as he handed his cloak to his thick-set butler. "Give her ladyship one of your special potions. Her ladyship has a bad cold. I won't keep you long, Lady Torrance."

He ushered Annie into a book-lined room and lit the gas-light in the gaselier and then the gas fire in the grate, which came alive with a loud, noisy pop.

"I shall be back presently," he said. "Do drink Hodder's remedy. There's nothing like it, I assure you."

After he had gone, Annie sat shivering by the fire and looked about her. It was a depressing room with heavy Victorian furniture and dusty birds in glass cases. The books were great tomes that looked as if they had never been opened. A heavy Wilton carpet covered an area of hard, shiny green linoleum. The lace undercurtains at the window were still dirty from the recent fog.

When Hodder came in bearing a tray, Annie looked at him uneasily, remembering his unlovely features from Britlingsea.

"It's a recipe I got from me mother," he said in a hoarse voice.

"What's in it?" asked Annie, taking the steaming cup.

"Just herbs and things like that. You'll feel ever so different after you've drunk it, my lady."

"Just leave me and don't loom over me, Hodder," said Annie. "Don't worry. I shall drink it. And thank you very much."

Hodder bowed and, to Annie's relief, withdrew. She found his personality strangely unpleasant.

She raised the cup to her lips but found that she could not drink it. Her stomach was beginning to feel upset with all that she had drunk at the ball. She looked around her, wondering what to do with it. There was a depressing-looking aspidistra in a brass bowl on a cane table. After some hesitation, she rose and dumped the contents of the cup into the earth around the plant.

After she had been waiting for ten minutes, she began to feel impatient. Part of her hurting mind wondered how she could even feel such a normal sensation as impatience when her heart was breaking and her temperature rising by the minute.

She rose to her feet, feeling a little giddy, and opened the door. The shadowy entrance hall was gloomy and deserted. She opened several doors but only found herself looking into dark, empty rooms. Then she heard a murmur of voices coming from downstairs.

Annie pushed open the green baize door that led to the kitchen quarters and walked down the stone steps.

The servants' dining room was lit by one lamp. Ahead of her, the kitchen door was closed. The voices were coming from there and, through the frosted glass of the upper part of the door, she could see the thin, predatory shadow of Mr. Shaw-Bufford confronting the squat shadow of the butler, Hodder.

She was just about to walk forward when she realized that the men were quarrelling, and hesitated, irresolute.

Then Hodder's gruff voice struck a chill into her heart. "Look here, guv'nor," he was saying. "This ain't goin' to be like gettin' rid o' that crazy woman, Hammond. I can't bump off a marchioness wiffout bringin' all the rozzers in London about me ears."

"Now, now, Hodder," came Mr. Shaw-Bufford's voice. "Haven't I explained that we will not be suspected? No one saw us leave except that fool Bellamy, and he can't remember anything from one minute to the next. I shall return to the ball as soon as possible.

That drug you gave her should have taken immediate effect. All you have to do is wrap her up in a blanket, tie those chains there around the body, and tip her into the Thames. Her marriage is unhappy. If by any chance the body is found – which it should not be, if you do your job properly – then it will be assumed that she committed suicide. Arrange the chains in such a way so that she could have put them around her herself."

"I dunno," said Hodder, doubtfully. "Member o' the peerage and all, and bein' connected, as you might say, wiff the Hammond murder . . . bound to smell somethin' awful."

"Nonsense, my good man. Did you get found out after the Hammond business? No. Did I? No. You are well paid, so go to it, man, and don't dither about."

"Very well, sir."

"And when you've finished your little chore, don't lock up. I shall be late. It's a pity we'll have to let Macleod live. I would dearly have liked to be prime minister. Women get equality, indeed! Why, you can't even trust one of them to carry out a simple shooting."

Somehow, Annie found herself turning and stumbling out of the kitchen. She thrust open the door into the hall and blundered toward the street door, knocking over a hat stand that hit the tiles with a tremendous crash.

All she wanted to do was find a policeman.

There was an alarmed shout from belowstairs.

The rain had stopped and a thin, ghostly mist wreathed the London streets. Annie kicked off her shoes with their Louis heels and ran for her life. Before she had turned the corner of the street, she heard Hodder's heavy feet pounding in pursuit.

Along Bradley Street, through Smith Square, fled Annie, too panic-stricken to stop and scream for help. She was desperate to reach the Houses of Parliament where she felt sure there would be a policeman on duty. She could hear Hodder's harsh breathing like that of some monster or wild animal.

Along Lord North Street ran Annie, down Peter Street, along Millbank and Abingdon.

Panic lending her wings, her shadow flying in front of her and then racing behind her as she passed under each gas lamp, Annie hurtled through St. Margaret's Square. Ahead lay Parliament Square and sanctuary in the shape of a possible constable on duty.

She had just reached the edge of Parliament Square when Hodder caught up with her and swung her around.

She kicked and scratched as Hodder fastened his huge hands around her neck.

Annie screamed for all she was worth. And then her voice was cut off by the murderously tightening fingers.

A red mist swam before her eyes. I will die and he'll never know how much I loved him, she thought as she clawed at the hands at her throat.

Then all at once there came the sound of horses' hooves, then a man's shouts. Hodder released her and she crumpled to the ground.

The Marquess of Torrance came hurtling toward the butler, who turned to face him. Hodder swung his fists wildly, but the marquess dodged and feinted and then slammed a vicious right straight to Hodder's chin. Hodder rocked on his heels, shook his head like a bull goaded by flies, and then rushed at the marquess, head down.

The marquess moved so fast that he seemed like a blur of black and white evening dress. One minute the butler was rushing toward him, and the next Hodder was hurtling through the misty air to land with a sickening thump against a lamp post. A police whistle shrilled through the damp cold.

The marquess poked Hodder's body with his foot to make sure that he was really unconscious, and then walked back and tenderly helped his wife to her feet, cradling her in his arms.

"Are you all right, Annie?" he whispered. "I was worried sick about you. Harry Bellamy said that you had left the supper room with Shaw-Bufford, and Dolly Bangor said that you looked ill. You weren't at home, so I decided you might have gone mad and gone to Shaw-Bufford's place, and, thank God, I came looking for you. Where is the chancellor? Who is that man who attacked you?"

"I'm surprised," said the Marchioness of Torrance, in a thin voice, "that you had time to think of me at all."

"Don't be silly . . ."

"Philandering with my sister . . ."

"Wot's all this then?" came the voice of the law.

"Philandering with . . . you little idiot!"

"Don't call me an idiot. Mr. Shaw-Bufford quite distinctly said that . . ."

"I must ask you to explain . . ." said the policeman, trying to interrupt.

"Oh, Jasper," wailed Annie, turning white as the full horror of the evening suddenly flooded over her. "Shaw-Bufford murdered Miss Hammond. Well, he didn't, but that's his butler, Hodder, and he did. And they

208

were trying to kill me."

The policeman's whistle was answered as several more officers of the law came pounding up.

"Wait there, Annie," said the marquess firmly. He drew the policemen a little way away and began to talk in a rapid voice. Two policemen went to put handcuffs on the still unconscious butler, and one more ran off for reinforcements.

There was a great deal of comings and goings. More constables arrived, headed by a squad of plainclothes detectives. Annie recognised Mr. Carton.

"Now, Annie," said the marquess. "Take the carriage and go home."

"No," said Annie stubbornly. "I must be there to accuse him. Otherwise he'll try to wriggle out of it."

"Let her ladyship come along," urged Mr. Carton. "When the chancellor sees her, he's bound to give himself up."

In silence they walked back along the way of Annie's flight. She picking up her discarded shoes as they turned the corner of Mr. Shaw-Bufford's street. Annie put her hand to her mouth. "I just remembered," she wailed. "He said he was going back to the ball."

"He may still be here," said Mr. Carton.

"Let's try the house first."

A constable, who had gone ahead, came back and said quietly, "The front door's open, sir."

"Good. Come along. Keep well behind us, your ladyship."

Back into the hall, into the dead quiet of the house.

"There's a light in the drawing room," whispered Annie. "The room I was in."

"Stand back," said Mr. Carton. He pushed open the door.

The chancellor was sitting at a desk in the corner. What was left of his head was lying on the blotter. A pearl-handled revolver lay beside him on the desk.

"That saves us some trouble," said Mr. Carton. "Mr Shaw-Bufford has done the decent thing."

It was then that Annie succumbed to a strong fit of hysterics. "The decent thing!" she shrieked, looking at the mess of blood and brains.

"Men!"

Chapter Eight

IT was jam for the newspapers. Murder in high places. Even the stately London *Times* blossomed forth with the headline: "The Butler Did It."

In the ensuing weeks before and after the trial, Annie felt that she was under a sort of house arrest. Reporters and cameramen lurked around every corner and she could not venture from the house without a magnesium flash going off in her face.

Marigold was furious and postponed the wedding, saying that she could not possibly get married while one of the family was disgracing herself by becoming embroiled in a murder trial.

Scotland Yard had unearthed Mr. Shaw-Bufford's past and had found that, at one time, the late chancellor had been confined to a mental asylum in Yorkshire. They kept this tidbit from the press since it would have started a tremendous scandal over the lack of national security.

As it was, Mr. Shaw-Bufford had unwittingly taken the prime minister down with him. Mr. Macleod was forced to resign. A prime minister who had had a murderer and a madman in his cabinet was not to be trusted.

211

Then the tactless Harry Bellamy had sparked an enormous row by proclaiming that Annie had been "tremendously brave." Marigold had called him a fool. Mr. Bellamy had called his beloved a shrew and before Marigold had time to collect her wits, the engagement was off, and the wedding presents were being returned.

Marigold, the Earl and Countess of Crammarth, and their retinue of servants departed for Scotland.

Annie found that you could be married to a man and live in the same house with him, yet hardly ever see him. Sometimes she saw him at the breakfast table, but his sunny good humor seemed to have disappeared completely, and when she tried to talk to him, he appeared to be too engrossed in the morning papers even to speak to her.

Becoming more and more depressed and insecure, Annie stopped worrying about her dress or her hair. She spent long hours reading novels as she used to do at Crammarth, hiding in a fantasy world, escaping from reality.

When she had thought that she was about to die, she had realized in one blinding flash how much she loved her husband. And that seemed to make things worse than ever before.

It was only when she realized that it was

nearly Christmas that she decided to venture out with her maid and do some shopping. The air was crisp and clear, and the sooty buildings were edged with white from a light snowfall the night before.

She poked about among the jewelry and objects d'art in Asprey's in Bond Street, trying to find something that would please her husband.

There were a number of fashionably dressed women in the shop talking in high, brittle voices.

All at once, Annie saw Dolly Bangor and turned quickly away, not wanting to be recognized.

She found herself looking at her own reflection in a pretty, gilt-framed looking glass.

Annie stared in amazement at her tired, drawn face and puffy eyelids. A lifeless strand of red hair had escaped from under her drab hat and was falling over her forehead.

"Lady Torrance!" came Dolly Bangor's voice, and Annie instinctively put a hand in front of her face – to hide herself from Dolly or to hide herself from herself, she wasn't quite sure.

Mrs. Bangor's glowing, dimpled face appeared in the looking glass behind Annie's shoulder as Annie slowly drew her hand away.

"Ooooh!" trilled Dolly. "Have you been ill? Silly me. It must have been all the strain of that terrible murder. Are you free? I'm simply dying to hear all the gory details!"

"I must go," said Annie abruptly. "Excuse me, Mrs. Bangor, I really must go."

She blundered from the shop and out into the street, leaving Dolly Bangor staring after her.

How crystal clear, how *alive* everything looked. A clerk walked by with his Christmas goose slung over his arm. The air smelled of smoke and roasting chestnuts and hot bread and coffee.

"Where to, my lady?" asked Barton timidly. She thought her mistress looked very strange.

"Home," said Annie. "Home, Barton, and you must put your genius to work on my appearance. I look like a frump. You might have told me."

"It wasn't my place to say anything of that nature, my lady," said Barton righteously. "Although I did keep offering to arrange your ladyship's hair, but my lady kept saying she would just 'shove it up on top of her head.' "

"I did, didn't I?" said Annie in a wondering voice. "I haven't even worked at *anything*. I don't think I've even *tried* to talk to him. I've only glared or whined."

"Who, my lady? Who? Him?" queried Barton, scurrying along the narrow pavement to try to keep up with her mistress.

But Annie had the awful realization that her husband had once loved her and that she had done everything she could to push him away.

Annie worked on her appearance the rest of the day.

By dinnertime, she was seated hopefully in the dining room. She was wearing a Merveilleuse dress, a revival of the fashion of the Empire period.

It bore little resemblance to the transparent, nymphlike creations of the Regency period, although it did consist of a chemise dress with a highish waistline, which gave a narrow look to the hips. A corset was worn underneath, as well as pantaloons trimmed with lace and petticoats of a soft, lightweight cotton called nainsook. It was in Annie's favorite color, pale leaf green. Once more her hair was burnished and shining. Her skin was delicately rouged, and she had daringly darkened her long lashes with lamp black.

But the marquess showed no signs of turning up to see all of this transformation.

He had not told the servants that he would not be home, so Annie waited dinner an hour for him, feeling her heart thud against her ribs every time a carriage rattled along the street outside. At last she had dinner on her own.

But there was still hope.

She sat in the drawing room, waiting, ever hopeful, trying not to run to the window every time she thought she heard him coming.

At last, with a little sigh, she trailed up to bed, all her newfound determination and courage gone.

Sadly, she allowed Barton to brush out the new hairstyle and prepare her for bed. She sat warming her toes at the bedroom fire and drinking the milk her maid had brought her.

Barton turned down the bed and said a quiet "Good night," and Annie was once more left alone.

But somehow she could not go back to that hopeless state. She found herself waiting and listening again. Waiting for her husband's return home.

At last she heard soft footsteps on the stairs and then they retreated along the corridor. It was either John, the second footman, making his late-night rounds or her husband going to bed.

Silence.

Annie could not bear it a minute longer. She must, simply must, find out what her husband felt for her. And if he felt nothing, well, then, they could get a divorce.

She opened her bedroom door and peeped out. A light was shining from the bathroom adjoining her husband's suite. The door to his suite was open, as was the bathroom door.

Wearing only a frivolous lilac nightdress, she walked along the corridor making as much noise as possible, not wanting to catch him undressing.

As she reached the bathroom door, her husband called out, "I say, John, I've dropped the sponge. Be a good fellow and get it for me."

Without pausing for thought, Annie walked into the bathroom. It was full of steam, and both the bath and her husband were hidden by a screen. The sponge was lying in the middle of the floor in a pool of water.

She picked it up and held it around the corner of the screen. The marquess stopped splashing in the bath.

Suddenly a strong hand clasped Annie's wrist and a strong arm pulled Annie around the screen.

"Well, my love," said the Marquess of Torrance. "And to what do I owe this sudden rush of, er, wifely intimacy?"

His hard-muscled body was glistening with water, and droplets of water clung to the black hairs on his chest. He was sitting in the bath, the sponge in one hand and Annie's wrist still held in the other.

Annie modestly averted her eyes. "I c-came to apologize, Jasper," she said in a low voice.

"Indeed! And what are you apologizing for?" His eyes were very blue and very bright, and fixed on her face.

Annie searched for words to describe her own feelings of inadequacy. To explain how she could never really feel that he had married her because of any feelings of affection. To explain that she feared that what Marigold had said about him might turn out to be true. Once a rake, always a rake.

Then she found herself saying, "For never having told you I love you."

"Oh, my love." He laughed. "You have been torturing and tormenting me for months. I thought you didn't care a rap for me! Oh, *Annie* . . ."

He gave her a hard pull so she toppled over into the bath on top of him.

Annie's mouth was imprisoned in a soapy kiss as he slid down on his side in the water and held her against him.

"Jasper," said Annie, desperately, "I must know why you married me."

"I don't know," he said, his face alive with

love and laughter. "I think it must have been because of the way your forehead wrinkles when you are worried."

"Oh, *Jasper*," wailed Annie.

"Of course, I also love you to distraction, if love is wanting to wring your neck most of the time." His voice suddenly became serious, intense. "But I wanted love in return, Annie. I did not want a woman who had taken me only to compete with her sister. Look at me! Let me see your eyes!"

He gazed down at her for a long moment and what he saw in her eyes made him crush her to him.

"Jasper," protested Annie, "you are drowning me!"

"Shut up! I'm loving you," said the Marquess of Torrance.

John, the second footman, saw the open bathroom door and the wet towels lying on the floor, went in, and bent to pick them up. Suddenly he looked at the bath and turned as red as a lobster and hurriedly backed out and fled to the kitchens.

"What's the matter, lad?" said Perkins, the butler. "Seen a ghost?"

"No, Mr. Perkins, sir. I went into the bathroom 'cos I saw all them wet towels lying on the floor. I was picking them up and then I saw *them*."

"Who's them?" asked the cook, pouring herself another glass of gin and water.

"My lord and my lady," said the footman. "There they was in the bath, going at it like a couple o'seals. T'ain't natural. What they got good beds for, that's what I want to know."

Perkins drew himself up and straightened his striped waistcoat.

"Bed for *you*, young man," he said sternly to the footman. "And don't let me hear you again, questioning the ways of your betters."

John went off to look for a more sympathetic audience. "Can't blame 'im," sniffed Mrs. Barnes, the cook. " 'E ain't used to the ways of the quality. 'Member Lord and Lady Chisholm, Mr. Perkins? Did it out in the shrubbery, back o' the house. But they never 'ad no children. I'll say one thing, though, it's 'igh time the master and mistress got together. And when you look at it, open-minded like, a bath's a nice, clean place!"

CATHERINE DARBY TITLES
IN LARGE PRINT

The publishers hope that this book has given you enjoyable reading. Large Print Books are especially designed to be as easy to see and hold as possible. If you wish a complete list of our books, please ask at your local library or write directly to: Magna Print Books, Long Preston, North Yorkshire, BD23 4ND England.

DEMCO